Books by T.A. Chase

Dracul's Revenge

Dracul's Blood
Anarchy in Blood

The Four Horsemen

Pestilence
War
Famine
Death
Peace

The Beasor Chronicles

Gypsies
Tramps

Home

No Going Home
Home of His Own
Wishing for a Home
Leaving Home
Home Sweet Home

International Men of Sports

A Sticky Wicket in Bollywood
Chasing the King of the Mountains
At First Touch
Blindsided
Burning Up the Ice

Serving Love at Carnival
A Grand Prix Romance
An Ace in the Tiebreak

Rags to Riches

Remove the Empty Spaces
Close the Distance
Following His Footsteps
Anywhere Tequila Flows
Walking in the Rain
Barefoot Dancing

Delarosa Secrets

Borderline
Snap Decision
Cold Truth

The Blood & Thorn Ranch

Bulls and Blood

Merging Violently

Fall into My Kiss

Every Shattered Dream

Every Shattered Dream: Part One
Every Shattered Dream: Part Two
Every Shattered Dream: Part Three
Every Shattered Dream: Part Four
Every Shattered Dream: Part Five

Sexy Snax

Two for One

Where the Devil Dances

What's His Passion?

What's His Passion?
Mountains to Climb
Climbing the Savage Mountain

Anthologies

Unconventional at Best
Unconventional in Atlanta
Semper Fidelis
An Unconventional Chicago
Unconventional in San Diego
Aim High

Single Titles

Out of Light into Darkness
The Haunting of St. Xavier
From Slavery to Freedom
The Vanguard
Ninja Cupcakes
Stealing Life
Lassoes and Lust
His Last Client
No Bravery
Always Ready
Possibilities
Ajay's Birthday Gift
The Unicorn Said Yes
Hearts on the Line

Borderline

ISBN # 978-1-78651-897-2

Interior text design by Claire Siemaszkiewicz

Pride Publishing

Published in 2016 by Pride Publishing, Newland House, The Point, Weaver Road, Lincoln, LN6 3QN, United Kingdom.

Pride Publishing is a subsidiary of Totally Entwined Group Limited.

Printed in Great Britain by Clays Ltd, St Ives plc
1

Delarosa Secrets

BORDERLINE

T.A. CHASE

Dedication

To all the men and women who fight to protect the innocent from the evil in the world.

Prologue

The knife sliced through her flesh like butter and he studied the glistening liquid that pooled from the wound in the dim lights of the warehouse. Her eyes widened from the pain and she tried screaming, but the gag in her mouth absorbed the sound.

He grinned as she struggled against her restraints. He enjoyed the ones who fought, who always believed they could escape. It was so much sweeter when they broke.

Another cut and more of that dark ruby liquid. God, how he loved the sight and smell of blood. Maybe one night he would drink it to see if it really did give him inhuman powers. At the moment, though, his interest lay in making the bitch bleed until her life drained from her.

Why had he never done this before? Oh, he'd killed before, but never with this kind of attention to detail and pain. It was exquisite, and he was going to want to do this again. Yet he needed to focus on the victim before him. She had to die, and he was going to be in control of when she did.

Chapter One

Macario Guzman stalked into the Houston headquarters of the Texas Rangers Company 'A'. Chaos reigned as he pushed his way through the seething crowd of reporters to reach his boss's office. Major Billingsley looked up when Macario tapped on his door.

"Good. You're finally here. Come with me."

Billingsley grabbed his hat and gun before shoving his way out through the mob.

"Couldn't you have told me to wait for you in the parking lot?" Macario growled as he sidestepped a precariously perched photographer.

"Didn't realize we were going anywhere until after I got off the phone with you." Billingsley's brisk Harvard accent was at odds with his Stetson and boots.

"Where are we going?" Macario removed his hat, scrubbing his hand through his hair before putting it back on.

Frustration and exhaustion warred inside him, and he resisted the urge to give Marissa another call. He hadn't talked to Marissa in close to two days. Normally that wouldn't have been a problem, but his foster sister had been troubled the last time they'd seen each other and Macario was worried about her.

Combining non-existent sleep with investigating the serial killer haunting the streets of Houston, Macario was running on fumes.

"We're going to the Bureau office." Billingsley grunted as he gestured for Macario to drive.

"Are they trying to muscle in on the case?" He climbed

behind the wheel of his non-descript tan sedan.

He had respect for the FBI and the agents who worked there, but sometimes he tended to think they were media whores. This serial killer case had shaped up to be quite a press frenzy. Something the Bureau always loved to be a part of.

"I asked them, Mac. Our profilers are good, but the Bureau has some of the best."

"I got ya, sir."

Macario understood. Jurisdiction didn't matter anymore. Not with four women dead and no real clues except their killer liked to use a knife. His stomach rolled at the thought of the most recent victim.

"You look like shit, Mac. What was the point of sending you home last night if you weren't going to sleep?"

Bringing up Marissa never crossed Macario's mind. No one at the Rangers knew anything personal about him and he wanted it that way. Ten foster homes in ten years had taught him to keep his mouth shut and any emotions hidden. It wasn't until he was fifteen and had been placed with the Levisten family that he'd had an inkling of what family could mean.

"I'll sleep when the case is over, sir." And when he finally talked to Marissa again.

They arrived at the Federal Building where the Bureau, along with several other government agencies, had their local offices. As they walked in, several men wearing DEA jackets rushed out.

"Hey, Mac," one of them yelled.

He turned to see a man peel away from the group. He grinned and shook the agent's hand.

"Snap. It's good to see you, man. What's going down?" Macario nodded at the convoy of black SUVs pulling up in front of the building.

"Just got a tip about Victor Delarosa being in town. We're planning on hitting a spot we think he might be." Snap shook his head. "More than likely he won't be there."

"Man's like a ghost. It's amazing how he manages to get away from everyone." Macario frowned.

"Almost like he has an in with the agency or something," Snap muttered.

Mac wouldn't have been surprised if they discovered Delarosa really did have a spy in several federal agencies.

"Snap, get your ass over here," one of the other guys ordered.

"Good luck. Give me a call. We'll play some poker together soon."

"Will do."

Billingsley and Macario watched the men leave before going through the metal detectors and heading up to the FBI offices.

"I feel sorry for those guys. They just keep chasing their tails with Delarosa."

"We're here to see Special Agent in Charge Samuel MacLaughlin. I'm Major James Billingsley and this is Ranger Macario Guzman from the Rangers."

The receptionist buzzed someone and repeated what Billingsley had told her. She nodded once before hanging up.

"Agent MacLaughlin will be right out."

"Thanks."

They didn't have to wait long.

"Major Billingsley." A booming voice ran through the lobby.

A large, red-faced, white-haired man strolled up to them with a big grin on his face.

"Agent MacLaughlin." Billingsley shook the man's hand. "Thanks for seeing us."

"No big deal. Always glad to help out fellow law enforcement. Come with me."

Macario kept his mouth shut as they wound their way through the central room where most of the agents' desks were. He nodded at a few agents he recognized from joint operations.

MacLaughlin waved them into his office. "So you're looking for some help on that serial killer case I've been hearing about."

"Yes, sir."

"Please, call me Sam. And you are?" Sam shot a glance at Macario.

"Ranger Macario Guzman. I'm the lead on the murders." He shook Sam's hand.

"Nice to meet you. Sit. Would either of you like some coffee? What can we do to help you out?"

Macario sat, but didn't say anything. Going to the FBI was his boss's idea and he wasn't about to take over.

"Yes. We'll both take some. It's been a helluva four months, Sam. Four women killed by the same guy. Sliced almost beyond recognition. We were hoping one of your profilers could take a look at the pictures and information we've gathered at the crime scenes. Just in case our guys missed something."

Sam stared off into the distance before blinking and giving a nod. He picked up the phone and pushed a button.

"Hey, Tanner, come in here and bring two cups of coffee with you." Sam listened for a moment. "I know you're busy. Just get in here."

After hanging up, Sam leaned back in his chair. "We'll wait until Tanner gets here before you tell me anymore about the case."

Billingsley accepted Sam's suggestion. "I see the DEA's got a hot tip about Delarosa."

"Won't matter. I doubt the man's wherever they think he is. He's as slippery as a snake."

Macario agreed with the agent. The Delarosa cartel ran a majority of the drugs out of Texas. His supply came through Mexico and his business was booming. No matter how much police and other law enforcement thought they knew, no one was able to pin anything on Victor Delarosa, the head of the empire.

"He's a tricky bastard," Billingsley commented.

"Enough to make you yank out your hair or become an alcoholic out of frustration." Sam grimaced in disgust.

The door opened.

"You shouldn't be drinking coffee and you know I hate the stuff."

Macario turned in his chair. Every atom in his body came to attention at the sight of the gorgeous man standing in the doorway. Unlike most of the Feds, the man's dark hair fell in curls to just above his shoulders. Golden skin attested to his Hispanic heritage. The agent glanced up and blushed.

"Sorry, boss. I didn't realize you had visitors with you. I would have knocked, but my hands are full."

Seeing the cups in the agent's hands, Macario jumped to his feet and took them from him. "I'll take those."

"Thanks."

When standing, they were the same height and build, and even though the agent seemed fit, like he worked out, there was a certain softness in his eyes. Almost like he hadn't seen how much pain humans could inflict on each other, but that didn't make sense if he was the profiler Sam had called. Bureau profilers saw the aftermath of some of the most horrific crimes.

"It's all right, Tanner. The coffee is for the Rangers and they're really here to see you." Sam waved a hand in their direction. "This is Major Billingsley and Ranger Macario Guzman. Gentlemen, this is Special Agent Tanner Wallace."

"Nice to meet you."

He and Tanner shook hands. Macario liked the strength of Tanner's grip. He wondered what it would feel like to have Tanner's hand wrapped around his cock. Okay, not an appropriate thought. At least not to have at work.

Only Billingsley knew Macario was gay. He'd told the major the first day he'd been assigned to the Houston office. It was better if one of his superiors knew—it kept him from being susceptible to blackmail. Yet none of the guys Macario worked with knew he liked men.

Tanner held his hand a little longer and Macario caught

a flash of interest in the guy's eyes. He filed it away for future inspection because exploring a new attraction in the middle of a case wasn't smart, especially if Tanner ended up working with them.

"I can go get cream and sugar if you guys want some." Tanner's smile included both Macario and Billingsley.

"I've learned to drink it black." Macario sipped his. "You can have my seat."

"Yes, sit down, Tanner. Billingsley wanted to consult with you on the recent string of murders they're dealing with."

Tanner frowned while he sat. "I thought the Rangers had their own profilers."

"We do, but I want a new pair of eyes, Agent Wallace. Anything you can give us will help, even if it's just supporting what my guy has said."

"Certainly, sir. I'll do what I can to help." Tanner glanced at Macario. "Please, call me Tanner."

Before Billingsley could say anything, the major's cell rang.

"Excuse me." He unclipped it and checked the number. "I have to take this. Mac, why don't you catch Agent Wallace up on our situation?"

Macario waited until Billingsley had left the room before he started talking.

"I'm pretty sure you've heard something about this. It's on all the local news channels and national media has latched on to it as well." He curled his upper lip in disgust at how the media vultures had descended on Houston. "Four women have been brutally murdered in the last four months. We're pretty sure the same man killed all four of them and our profiler agrees."

Tanner and MacLaughlin nodded.

"The media has nicknamed him 'The Knife', which will only encourage him, I'm sure, but it sells papers and gets ratings. It doesn't hurt that he's a master in using a blade."

"Before you tell me anymore, can I see the photos? I'd like to form my own profile first, after which we'll compare them to see if they match."

"That works for me." Macario pointed to the folder Billingsley had set on MacLaughlin's desk. "Those are copies of all the photos."

Billingsley stuck his head in the office. "Mac, you have to head out. We got a call about a possible homicide."

"Is it our guy?" He stood.

Billingsley shrugged. "They didn't know. Just that it might be."

"Okay. I'm on my way."

Tanner stood as well. "I'll go with you. If it's another knife murder, seeing a fresh scene will help me get more ideas about your suspect."

Macario looked at Billingsley and his major nodded.

"Fine with me. Can you drive? I rode over with Billingsley."

"Yes."

Macario followed Tanner from the Bureau's offices. His eyes were drawn to Tanner's ass, catching glimpses of the jean-clad flesh. He blinked, raising his gaze to Tanner's board shoulders.

"I thought Feds wore suits," he commented as they reached a dark blue sedan.

Tanner grinned. "Oh, we do, but I tend to operate on my own dress code. Sam doesn't mind as long as I do my job."

Macario chuckled. "I guess you must be good at your job."

"Where are we headed?"

Tanner pulled out of the parking garage while Macario checked his phone. Billingsley had emailed him the information.

"Nine-eight-seven-nine Thurston Street. You know where that is?"

"Yep. I've lived in Houston all my life." Tanner sent him a quick glance. "How about you?"

"Moved here about ten years ago when I got my job with the Rangers. Originally from California."

"You must like it here, since you've stayed that long."

"Probably like it a lot better if my job wasn't dealing with crime and dead people." Macario stared out of the passenger window at the people flashing by.

"Isn't that the truth?" Tanner turned left, bypassing a lot of downtown traffic. "What do you do for fun when you're not working a case?"

"Watch sports. I play on a softball league." He went out on a limb. "Go to Windy's for drinks once in a while."

Windy's was the biggest gay club in Houston. Maybe he was taking a risk by admitting he went there, but the interest he'd seen in Tanner's eyes had told him he'd be okay mentioning it.

"I've been there a couple times. Not big on clubs. They tend to be really crowded and I don't like crowds."

That had gone well, so Macario took a step he rarely took with other law enforcement men.

"Maybe we could go someplace quieter for drinks and dinner sometime?" he suggested.

He got a bright smile from Tanner.

"I'd like that."

They pulled up in front of a warehouse and climbed out of the car. Several police cars lined the street and the medical examiner's van was already there. Macario headed toward the door, figuring Tanner would follow. He held up his badge for the uniform at the entrance.

"He's with me." He gestured at Tanner who flashed his own badge at the guy.

"No problem, sir. Nothing's been touched. We were told to wait until you arrived."

"Thanks."

He hurried down the echoing hallway to where people had gathered in the doorway of a room.

"Sorensterm, what do you have?"

His fellow Ranger and occasional work partner looked up, his face even paler than usual. "It's another victim, Mac. No way it can't be."

Macario steeled himself before he glanced in the room. Staring at the body so obscenely displayed, he accepted the gloves and booties for his shoes from one of the crime scene techs. The victim's blonde hair streaked with blue caught his attention and his heart stopped.

God, it couldn't be. Please don't let it be. He wanted to rush over to check the victim, but in the deepest part of his heart, he knew.

Once he was outfitted to go in without contaminating the scene, he entered and went directly to the body. His hands trembled as he angled his head to see the inside of the woman's elbow. A birthmark marred the skin and Macario closed his eyes.

He swallowed his shout of anger and clenched his hands. While every muscle and nerve in his body wanted to tear something apart, he forced all his emotions behind a door in his mind. He'd deal with everything later when he was by himself.

No one could know he knew the killer's latest victim. He didn't want to get taken off the case, especially now that he had an even stronger reason to solve it.

Marissa, his foster sister, was dead.

* * * *

Standing in a corner, out of the crime techs' way, Tanner committed everything to memory. The photos would help jog them when he reviewed the file, but he was happy to see a fresh scene. He winced. Okay, so happy wasn't the best choice of words. No one could be happy at the carnage done to the female. Yet being able to see it firsthand would help him get inside the mind of the killer.

He glanced over at Ranger Guzman. Something was bothering the man, and had been since they'd arrived at the warehouse. Whatever it was went deeper than just having a fifth victim. Tanner studied Macario's body language. The tense shoulders, clenched hands, and the way he watched every move the techs made spoke to it being more than just a good detective wanting everything done by the book.

As one of the techs lifted the victim's arm, it slipped from her hand to drop with an audible thud on the table where the woman had been displayed.

"Show some respect," Macario barked.

The tech's expression questioned his order, giving Tanner a hint that Macario wasn't normally so harsh.

"Please be more careful and mark any postmortem bruising," Tanner spoke up, giving the woman a request that made sense to her.

Macario blinked like he'd forgotten Tanner was there then nodded at him before approaching the medical examiner. Tanner moved closer as well.

"What you got for me, Doc?"

The ME grunted. "I put time of death about twelve hours ago."

"Just like the others," Macario muttered.

"It appears so. I'll be able to tell you more after the autopsy." The ME frowned impatiently at Macario. "You finished? Can I take her?"

Macario looked at Tanner, who nodded. The crime photographer had been thorough and Tanner figured he'd have enough different angles to recreate the scene if necessary.

A body bag was brought in and Macario hovered like he was afraid the techs would drop her. Tanner wanted to make a comment about the woman being dead. She wouldn't know if they did. With the way Macario was acting, Tanner figured the detective wouldn't find it funny.

Tanner respected death, but he didn't see the point of acting like the dead could hear or feel. Whatever sort of soul their bodies housed disappeared the minute their hearts stopped beating.

"Make sure every thing's bagged and logged in as evidence." Macario stalked from the room.

Tanner looked over his shoulder as he left. They were

settling the body onto the gurney. Something on her chest above her left breast caught his eye. The black bag covered most of it, and he made a mental note to check it out on the photos when he got them.

"Who called this in, Sorensterm?" Macario asked the other Ranger.

"Anonymous tip. More than likely some squatter or homeless person found her and called it in. Maybe they thought they'd get a reward or something." Sorensterm shrugged.

"Another anonymous tip." Macario shook his head.

"The other bodies were found the same way?" Tanner inquired, seeing an upsetting and long afternoon in his future, getting caught up on the case.

"Yes. Each coming twelve hours after the girl was killed. Who are you?" Sorensterm eyed him.

"Special Agent Tanner Wallace. I'm a profiler with the Behavioral Science Unit, but I'm assigned to the Houston branch of the Bureau."

"Jasper Sorensterm, detective, Texas Rangers. I occasionally work cases with Mac." Jasper's grim expression got even darker as the gurney rolled by. "So Major Billingsley decided to bring in the big guns."

Macario nodded, but didn't say anything, not taking his gaze off the black bag being loaded into the truck.

"What I believe is that your boss decided to get a second opinion—or profile—on your killer. To see how accurate the first one was. As far as my boss is concerned, we'll offer assistance, but this is your show," Tanner interjected.

"Awfully nice of you." Sorensterm didn't look convinced.

Tanner shrugged. He didn't really care whether Sorensterm believed him or not. He didn't play office politics and he sure as hell wasn't going to play inter-agency games either. He would do his job as Sam directed him and pray they caught the bad guy before the bastard killed again.

"Hey, Mac, I've been trying to get a hold of Snap to

set up our next poker game. You hear from him today?" Sorensterm changed the subject.

"Saw him at the Federal Building. Him and his team were heading out to pick up Victor Delarosa."

Sorensterm froze in surprise and Tanner barely suppressed his own shock at the mention of Delarosa.

"You're not serious?"

Macario rolled his eyes. "Do you really think this time is going to be any different than the dozens of times they've gone before? No matter how good the tip is, Delarosa won't be there. Guy has an intel network that rivals the CIA. He's always twelve steps ahead of us. I'm getting to the point where I don't think anyone will catch the man unless he wants them to. Or he's dead."

Tanner shifted slightly. Any talk about Delarosa made him nervous and he didn't want to hear about Delarosa being dead. Macario suddenly seemed to remember Tanner was there.

"Tanner, you're welcome to canvas the area with us, or you can go back to your office and start looking at the photos. I can catch you up on the other killings later."

As much as he wanted to stay with Macario, he wasn't really needed.

"I'll go back then. Call me when you have time to talk."

He tipped his head to both men before strolling to his car. He felt someone's gaze on him and hoped it was Macario. The Texas Ranger was as tall as Tanner and their builds were similar, but where Tanner got his muscles from the gym, he had a feeling that Macario got his from playing sports and outdoor activities.

Macario's dark brown hair was cut ruthlessly short. His odd golden-hazel eyes were cool and observant, yet Tanner wouldn't have been surprised to find out the man hid a passionate nature under his chilly exterior.

After he started his car, he risked looking back. Sorensterm had disappeared, but Macario stood there, watching the car intently. Tanner lifted a hand and Macario responded by touching his fingertips to the brim of his hat.

"Whew, Tanner my boy. I do believe you're in over your head," he muttered as he drove away.

Knowing he shouldn't, he dug out his personal cell phone and punched in a number.

"No worries," the deep voice answering the phone told him.

"Thank you." He hung up, tossing the phone on the passenger seat next to him. It was stupid to call because he risked everything by doing so, but he needed to know. At times, the worry kept him up at night and he hated it.

He arrived back at the offices, just in time to watch the DEA agents return.

"No luck?" He stepped onto the elevator with a large African-American agent.

"No." The man shook his head and smiled weakly. "Never thought he'd be there. Told my boss we needed to get reliable proof before we rallied the troops. No one listens to me."

"Sorry to hear it didn't work."

"No big deal. We're still cutting into his supply chain and his money. Only be a matter of time before we trip him up."

The DEA agent got off on his floor, and Tanner rode up one more before stepping off.

"Agent Wallace, Special Agent MacLaughlin would like to see you asap," the receptionist passed on the request.

"Thanks, Susie."

He wandered down the hallway to Sam's office. He knocked and waited for the gruff 'come in' before entering.

"Susie said you wanted to see me."

"Yes. Sit." Sam pointed to a chair. "I wanted to talk to you about this serial killer case."

"Okay." He found it best to let Sam do most of the talking.

"I want you to stay on top of things with that detective. Make sure he keeps you in the loop as much as possible."

"I thought we weren't taking over the case." Tanner frowned.

"We're not at the moment, but if the time comes for us to step in and take the lead, I don't want there to be any lag time while we're getting up to speed." Sam exhaled loudly. "This is a bad case. One of the worst I've seen. The insane asshole butchers them, Tanner. He tortures and slowly lets them bleed to death from their wounds."

"And displays them in a macabre, five-pointed star position."

"Do you think he's a devil worshipper?" Sam was cautious about saying that.

Tanner knew his boss didn't want to plant suggestions in his head, but Tanner's mind had already gone there.

"It's one possibility. I'll have to learn more about the victims. There's a reason why he's picking the women he takes."

"Of course." Sam waved his beefy hand at the door. "Copies of all the files were delivered while you were out. Start going through them. Hopefully you'll find something to help."

Tanner stood. "I'll do my best, sir."

Before heading to his office, Tanner detoured to the break room where he made some tea. He'd drunk so much coffee when he'd started out at the Bureau, he'd ruined his stomach. Now he couldn't drink the stuff, which was for the best. The caffeine wasn't good for him either. Cup of tea in hand, he returned to his office to find two boxes on the small table joined to his desk.

"Should've brewed more tea," he said aloud as he set his mug down.

He hung up his jacket, loosened his tie then rolled up his sleeves. Time to do his job, no matter the cost to his soul.

Chapter Two

Macario stared out of the window of his apartment at the dog park it overlooked. He wasn't seeing the animals or their owners. Memories of Marissa raced through his head. He'd only lived with her family for six months before Mr. Levisten had been transferred out of California and Mac had been sent back into the system.

When he'd turned sixteen, he'd run away from his last foster home and had lived on the streets until José Guzman had taken him in. The elderly Hispanic man had owned a grocery store and, for the first time since the Levistens, Macario had understood what family meant. José had adopted him and helped him make something of himself.

Macario had joined the California State Police fresh out of the academy. After José had decided to return to his native Texas, Macario had applied to and been accepted by the Texas Rangers. It was only by a twist of fate that he'd run into Marissa and they'd renewed their friendship.

Now that was over and he had to find a way to break it to her parents. He should be chasing down leads and trying to identify Marissa's killer, but for tonight, he was going to take the time to remember her the way she was and not how the bastard had left her.

He played back in his mind all the different moments he'd spent with Marissa when they were young, and more recently. They were the happiest times in his life. Macario had never been able to make friends easily because of how often he'd been shuffled from one home to another. Once Child Protective Services had taken him, he hadn't trusted anyone.

Marissa had ignored all of his walls and forced him to accept her friendship. Now she was gone, and he'd never see her smile or hear her laugh again. He clenched his empty hand, vowing he'd find the guy who killed her and bring him to justice.

As he took another sip of Scotch, his doorbell rang. He frowned while making his unsteady way to the door. He'd been drinking since he'd got home. Of course, he'd be no good to anyone if they got another murder.

"Who is it?"

"Tanner Wallace." The voice drifted through the barrier between them.

Fuck. What was the agent doing there? Macario had figured he wouldn't see the guy until the morning. Him showing up when Macario was half-drunk wasn't a good sign. It definitely wouldn't inspire confidence in his professionalism. He rested his forehead against the wall and sighed.

"Are you okay?"

Did Tanner know Macario wasn't handling this latest murder well? Hell, for all Tanner knew, this was how Macario reacted to all his cases. He could be an alcoholic, just marking his days until he could retire. That didn't make any sense since at thirty-one Macario had another ten or fifteen years before he called it quits.

He unlocked the door then strolled back to his spot by the window, stopping to refill his glass on the way. Footsteps behind him informed him that Tanner had come in.

"Who was she?"

Tanner's soft question surprised Macario and he whirled, sloshing liquor over his hand.

"Who was who?" He tried to sound confused.

"This last victim. You knew her." Tanner shrugged out of his leather jacket and hung it over the back of a chair.

Macario devoured the man with his gaze, trying not to drool at the lust-inducing sight Tanner made. The agent wore faded worn jeans that fit him like a glove. A long-sleeved, dark blue Henley graced Tanner's upper half, showing off a well-muscled chest and a flat stomach.

"No one," Macario muttered, keeping up his façade.

Tanner walked up to him and cradled his face with his hands. Shock held Macario still. No one touched him without his permission. Yet he had no inclination to yell at Tanner or back away from him.

"I promise to keep your secret, Macario, because God knows, I have my own. It might make you feel better to tell someone about her." Tanner glanced down at the glass in Macario's hand. "Instead of drinking your problems into oblivion."

If he was the kind of man who didn't take responsibility for his actions, he'd blame what he did next on the alcohol. Macario set his glass down and rested his hands on Tanner's hips. He leaned forward to bring their lips together.

Tanner gasped, and Macario took advantage of it to sweep his tongue inside Tanner's mouth, tasting the man. Spicy, like Tanner had had Tex-Mex for dinner, and a beer. There was a unique flavor that had to be all Tanner. They moaned and stepped closer until their bodies pressed tightly together, chest to chest, knee to knee, and groin to groin.

In the back of his alcohol-addled mind, Macario knew what they were doing wasn't smart. Messing with a man he was working with could screw everything up, but he couldn't bring himself to care.

He tugged on the hem of Tanner's shirt, lifting it so he could run his hands over Tanner's warm, smooth skin. Tonight he wanted to fuck and reinforce the fact that he still lived. It was the emotion that often swept over him when catching a murder case. Yet when he'd left work, he'd driven home instead, somehow feeling like it was disrespecting Marissa's memory to fuck some total stranger.

Isn't that what you're doing now? He pushed away the voice inside his head. Macario didn't want to think any more about what had happened that day. The alcohol was helping him to dull the pain, and maybe sex would help him get some sleep.

Tanner eased back, breaking the kiss. "Where's your bedroom?"

Macario grabbed the man's hand and dragged him down the hallway. He didn't speak, not wanting to break the mood. No coming to their senses until after they fucked. They could regret it in the aftermath.

You're such a playboy. Marissa's voice danced through his head, and Macario skidded to a halt without warning. Tanner slammed into his back with a grunt.

"What's wrong?" Tanner tightened his grip on Macario's hand.

"We can't do this." Macario turned to look at him. "I'm sorry."

Tanner laughed softly. "It might give me blue balls, but I think I can deal with it. You're trying to reaffirm that you're alive. Happens to those of us around death all the time. Are you the type to go to the bars and pick up a one-night stand?"

Macario dipped his head in embarrassment. More often than not, he'd done it, but not lately. Maybe his age was catching up to him, or after reconnecting with Marissa, he'd found he wanted more than quick anonymous sex.

He closed his eyes against the tears. Marissa, so beautiful and alive the last time he'd seen her. Teasing him about his revolving bedroom door. No more laughter. No more late-night phone calls to talk about her day. Macario bit his lip to keep from sobbing. The alcohol hadn't been a good idea. His control was slipping and he didn't want Tanner to see him weak and emotional.

"Why didn't you do that tonight?" Tanner led him back down the hall to the living room, and pushed him down onto the couch.

He laid his head back and stared up at the ceiling. "Because I couldn't face all those people and the fact that they're still fucking alive, and those five women are dead." He wasn't about to tell Tanner the real reason why he didn't.

"Okay." Tanner didn't join him on the couch. The agent sat in the chair opposite Macario. "But you've done it before with other homicides. Why not this one? What makes this one different?"

No way was he going to spill his guts to Tanner. It didn't matter that not five minutes ago he'd been ready to fuck the man's brains out. He didn't know Tanner and didn't trust him not to tell Billingsley that Macario knew one of the victims.

"Just tired, is all. It's been a long four months, always anticipating another murder. Never knowing when it'll happen. Not being able to tell women to be safe because we don't know anything about the killer except that he likes knives." Macario clenched his hands to get them to stop trembling.

Silence built in the room until he couldn't take it anymore. Lifting his head, he peeked through his eyelashes to find Tanner staring at him. The agent had pressed his fingertips together and rested them on his chin, just like a psychologist Macario had gone to see once used to do. Christ, Tanner was psychoanalyzing him now.

"I used to be married, you know." He threw out that bit of bait, hoping to distract Tanner from why this case was so different from the others.

"Really?" Tanner straightened slightly in his chair. "What happened?"

"She divorced me. Decided being married to a gay cop wasn't her thing." He scowled as he remembered that particularly nasty time in his life.

Tanner grimaced. "Sorry to hear that, but you didn't know you were gay when you married her, did you?"

"I suspected, but you know, I couldn't be a cop and be gay. I grew up in a macho family. I couldn't break my father's heart by not marrying someone. So I picked a girl and we got married. She had me figured out real quick, though." Macario went back to staring at the ceiling.

"Didn't end well?"

He shook his head. "Hell no. Only good thing was José was gone by then, so he didn't watch her drag me through the dirt."

"How long have you been divorced?"

Macario heard the rustle of fabric and knew Tanner was getting comfortable. Shit, now they were having a heart-to-heart. Sliding, he ended up on his side, meeting Tanner's amused gaze.

"Is it time for me to go?"

"I don't care. I'll probably fall asleep right here, but if you want to chat until we do, I'm game. I've been divorced for five years. She filed for divorce three days after José's funeral. During that time, I've fucked every willing man I could find. Had to make up for lost time, I guess." He rubbed his cheek against the smooth suede of the couch. "Not proud of it, but not going to lie about it either."

Tanner's smile was gentle and understanding in a way. "I get that."

The agent seemed about to say something else when his phone rang. Macario watched as Tanner tugged it out of his pocket and checked the number.

"I have to go."

Disappointment swept through Macario. He gave himself a mental slap. First, he complained about having a late-night chat with the man. Now, he was pissed because Tanner had to go.

"Got a boyfriend checking up on you?"

Tanner paused in the process of tucking in his shirt. He shot Macario an irritated glance. "Do you really think I'd kiss you if I had a boyfriend?"

Macario lifted his shoulder a little. "Probably not. You don't seem like the cheating kind."

"Not even remotely." Tanner crouched next to the couch and brushed his hand over Macario's hair. "Try not to fall asleep on the couch. It doesn't look that comfortable. I'll see you tomorrow."

Macario closed his eyes and accepted the kiss Tanner placed on his brow. He waited until after the door had shut behind Tanner before getting up to stagger over to lock up. After making sure the cap was back on the Scotch, Macario made his way to the bathroom where he took a hot shower.

He dried off then hung up the towel. Wandering back to his bedroom, he thought about how the night could have ended differently. Instead of sleeping alone, he could have wrapped up around Tanner, and maybe then the nightmares wouldn't haunt him.

Macario slipped under the blankets and curled up with one of his pillows. Not the same as a hot, hard body, but he'd learned to deal with the loneliness. He shut his eyes and breathed deeply, trying to relax enough to fall to sleep, though he knew he wouldn't get a full night of rest.

* * * *

"Macario, why didn't you save me?"

Marissa's sparkling eyes slowly went blank and dark as blood cascaded down over her skin, bathing her in dark ruby liquid. He knelt beside her, trying to stop her life from flooding out onto the floor.

"I'm sorry, Marissa. I'm so sorry. I didn't know he'd come after you."

He watched in horror as her flesh disintegrated, leaving a leering skeleton. His stomach turned as maggots and worms crawled from her mouth. A ringing noise entered the room he crouched in, and he glanced around.

The nightmare faded away as he swam toward consciousness. The guilt he felt at Marissa's accusing stare lingered, even as he sat up in his bed and reached for the phone next to it.

"Guzman."

"Get in here. We ID'd the last vic." Sorensterm sounded chipper and Macario hated him for that.

"When?" Macario dragged his ass out of bed then

stumbled to his dresser where he dug out a pair of clean briefs and socks.

"About five minutes ago. Her fingerprints were on file because she worked in the county clerk's office for year or two."

That was the job Marissa had held before she'd started working at one of the nightclubs. She'd wanted something with more excitement than filing permits all day. Macario had teased her about being a gypsy, never settling down. She'd laughed and told him she had the rest of her life to settle, but while she was young, she wanted to live. He swiped the tears from his eyes.

"Good. Send me the information on the parents. I'll go give them the news."

"Sure you don't want me or your FBI guy to go with you?"

Macario shook his head before realizing Sorensterm couldn't see him. "Nah. No point in ruining everyone's day. I hate informing the family, but it needs to be done."

"Better you than me, Mac. I can't take the crying." Clicking sounded. "I'm emailing you the address and name right now. I'll tell Billingsley where you are." Sorensterm hung up.

Macario snapped his phone shut and resisted the urge to chuck it against the wall. He dropped to sit on the edge of the bed, dangling his socks and underwear between his legs as he stared at the floor. *Christ!* It just wasn't fair that Marissa's life had been cut short. She was a good person and definitely hadn't deserved to die like that.

He took a shower and got dressed, taking special care to look nice. He even wore a suit because Marissa's parents had been good to him while he'd stayed with them, and he needed to show them some respect. As he drove to the address Sorensterm had sent him, he kept his mind blank. He never rehearsed what he was going to say to the families. Each circumstance was different because each family reacted differently to death. Of course, he'd never had to tell someone he knew that their daughter was dead.

Macario parked his car in the driveway and sat, staring at the modest ranch-style home. It had been sixteen years since he'd seen the Levistens. He and Marissa might have reconnected, but he hadn't been ready to see her parents. Not that he was ready now.

"What a shitty way to come back into each other's lives," he muttered.

Straightening his shoulders, he turned off the car and climbed out. He settled his suit coat over his gun. Before he took a step, his phone rang. Relief coursed through him at putting the conversation off even for a minute.

"Guzman."

"Macario, its Tanner Wallace. I wondered if you would be able to meet with me. I'd like to go over some things about the case."

His first reaction was to scream 'fuck no', but it was his emotions saying that, not his professionalism. A deep mental sigh calmed him down, as did the promise of a bottle of tequila when he finally made it home.

"Sure. Where do you want to meet?"

"Why don't you come to my place for dinner? That way we'll both get food and I can have a beer."

Not a good idea. Macario's rational brain shouted, but his cock thought being someplace private with Tanner sounded great.

"Sure."

He'd always been a glutton for punishment.

"Great. Anything you don't like or are allergic to?"

Macario snorted softly. Growing up a foster kid, he'd learned to never complain about what he ate. That often led to not getting food at all.

"I'll eat pretty much anything."

Tanner's chuckle socked Macario low in the gut.

"My kind of man," Tanner joked.

I wish. Again, so not appropriate, but Macario needed something to take his mind off the grim task before him. The front door of the Levisten house opened and Macario swore.

"What's wrong?"

"I have to notify the latest victim's family," he explained, "and I'm standing in their driveway now."

"That's sucks, man, especially since you know her and everything."

He gritted his teeth for a second before saying, "What makes you think I know them?"

"I saw how you reacted at the crime scene and afterward at your apartment. I'm making an educated guess."

"Mind your own damn business, Wallace." Macario snarled before he snapped his phone shut on the man. "Shit. Great way to make Tanner drop the subject, asshole." Macario shook his head as he muttered to himself.

He looked up to see Marissa's mother and father standing on the front porch, their eyes fixed on him. Even from the distance he stood away, he could see that Mrs. Levisten had been crying. Macario threw his shoulders back and headed up the walk.

"Mr. and Mrs. Levisten, I'm Detective Macario Guzman with the Rangers." He held out his badge for Marissa's father to check out.

"Macario?" Mrs. Levisten let go of her husband and threw herself into Macario's arms. "Marissa said she had found you and you had dinner once or twice."

He stood helplessly while she hugged him, unsure how to handle it all. "Ummm…yes. We did. Marissa's the reason why I'm here."

"Come on, honey. Let go of Macario and we can go inside." Mr. Levisten met Macario's eyes over the head of his wife and the pain in the man's eyes informed Macario that Marissa's father knew the truth.

"Oh, right. Have you heard from Marissa? We haven't heard from her in four days. That isn't like her. Usually she calls me once a day."

Macario allowed her to babble as he followed the couple into their house. It was neat, but looked lived-in, unlike

Macario's apartment that was almost as empty as it had been when he'd moved in.

"Please, sit. Can I get you something to drink?" Mrs. Levisten hovered and Macario shook his head.

"I think you and Mr. Levisten need to sit, ma'am."

The serious tone of his voice stopped her in her tracks and she wrung her hands while avoiding his gaze. Mr. Levisten took her arm and tugged gently, encouraging her to sit next to him on the couch. Macario took the chair across from them. He cleared his throat, debating how to start.

"Marissa's dead, isn't she, Macario?" Mr. Levisten's low voice cut through Macario's chest, piercing his heart with sorrow.

He nodded. "I'm sorry."

Mrs. Levisten screamed in agony and crumbled in her husband's arms. He held her close, pressing her face into his chest while tears fell from his eyes. After standing, Macario moved to the window, unable to block out the hearts breaking behind him. He rubbed his face and wished for the first time that he wasn't a cop. Informing families was difficult at the best of times, but he'd never hurt as badly as he did with this one.

Whispers behind him brought him around to see Mr. Levisten practically carrying his wife out of the room.

"Let me go get Jane settled and make a phone call. Can you wait until I get back? I want to hear the rest."

"I'm not sure you do, sir," Macario confessed.

"Marissa was my daughter, Macario. I wanted to be a part in all aspects of her life, and now that means her death as well."

Macario dipped his head, honoring Mr. Levisten's right to know everything about his daughter's death, except the things Macario couldn't tell him. Law enforcement would keep undisclosed clues from the press to stop copycat killers from using them to their advantage.

His phone beeped as Mr. Levisten led his wife down the hall to the back of the house. Macario assumed they were going to the bedroom. He pulled his phone out and saw he had a text.

U ok?

It came from Tanner's phone and the knowledge that the FBI agent cared enough to check on him warmed Macario in a way nothing had in a long time.

Rather get shot than b here.

Don't blame u. Have beer cold when u get here.

Macario's hands trembled slightly and he knew he needed something stronger than beer.

Make it tequila.

A minute went by before Tanner returned his text.

After the day u've had so far, tequila it is. C u later.

K. Thx.

He slipped his phone into his pocket and returned to staring out of the window. The neighborhood was quiet and middle class. The kind of place a girl like Marissa grew up. Marissa wasn't the girl who got murdered by a serial killer. She was a nice girl. Sure, she got drunk once in a while and got a little loud at times, but her behavior wasn't usually risky.

How did the bastard pick his victims? It was one thing they couldn't figure out. There didn't seem to be any sort of connection between them. Did the killer wander all over Houston and randomly pick his next victim? His MO during the actual murder stayed the same. All the stuff leading up to it seemed to change with each kill.

Macario hoped Tanner figured something new out from the scene photos. They needed more clues to work from, because if they didn't have them, there would be a sixth victim within the next three weeks. He didn't think he could deal with another one, not after seeing Marissa like that.

A soft cough behind him got his attention and he swung around. Mr. Levisten sat on the couch, hands clasped together and eyes red from his tears.

"Please tell me what happened to my daughter, Macario."

Taking a deep breath, Macario drew his courage and strength tight. He needed all of it to get through the upcoming conversation. He returned to his seat and perched on the edge, resting his elbows on his knees.

"There are some things I can't discuss with you, Mr. Levisten. In the on-going investigation, it's vital that certain things don't get out to the public."

Mr. Levisten nodded. "I understand. Was Marissa a victim of that serial killer the press has been talking about the last couple of months?"

"We can't be a hundred percent sure until all the results are in, but we believe so. She was found yesterday and her fingerprints came up in the computer. That's how we knew who she was so soon." Macario stiffened his backbone and met Mr. Levisten's devastated gaze. "I'll find who did this to Marissa and I'll put him in jail."

"No dark promises to kill him?"

Macario shook his head. "It might make us all feel better if he was to die, but it won't really be justice. I don't believe in 'an eye for an eye'. All that does is lead to more sorrow. Let us handle this and I promise we will find him."

Marissa's father looked at him with eyes the same color as Marissa. "I believe you, Macario, and thank you for coming over to tell us personally. I know this isn't the most enjoyable part of the job."

Macario snorted. "At times, there are no parts of this job I enjoy."

"When can we get the body released to us? We need to start planning the funeral."

After standing, Macario reached for the inside pocket of

his coat. "Here's my card. Call me if you have any questions, and I'll let you know as soon as I can about when you can get Marissa."

Mr. Levisten stood as well and, after setting the card on the coffee table, held out his hand to Macario. "As strange as this may sound, Macario, I'm glad you're the one on the case. We might not have had anything to do with each other for years, but I still feel like I know you. You'll keep your promise and we'll get justice for Marissa."

"Yes, sir."

They shook hands and Macario felt like he'd just sealed a vow with the handshake. They went to the front door and before Macario left, Mr. Levisten rested his hand on Macario's shoulder.

"Macario, I wish we had taken you with us all those years. It hurt all of us to leave you behind." The older man shook his head.

Macario shrugged. "I understood why you did it and it all worked out in the end. It was rough going, but I found a family."

Of sorts. José Guzman hadn't been the perfect father, but the elderly man had done his best to keep Macario from running the streets and getting into any more trouble. He'd given Macario a last name that meant something instead of one he hated with every atom in his body.

"I'm glad you and Marissa had a chance to find each other again. She often wondered what you were doing. You were the older brother she never had."

Mr. Levisten choked back a sob and Macario knew it was time to leave. Grief had started to take Marissa's father over. Macario didn't need to be there when the man broke down.

"I'll call as soon as they release her body."

"Thank you again," Mr. Levisten shut the door behind Macario.

Trudging to his car, Macario thought about getting a different job. Maybe he could be a security guard at a mall, or something like that. A job that didn't involve telling people their loved ones were victims of a violent crime. Shaking his head, he slid behind the wheel. He started the vehicle then pulled out of the driveway, going back to his office.

Chapter Three

Tanner rubbed his sweaty palm on his jeans and glanced around his dining room. Nice dishes, not his fancy stuff, and good silverware. No candles or any other romantic objects to make it look like he was trying to seduce the Ranger, even though he'd wanted Macario since the moment he first saw him.

Normally Tanner was good about not mixing business with pleasure. He'd met a lot of handsome men while doing his job, but Macario Guzman got under his skin in a way none of the others had.

With a small smile, Tanner laughed warily. He needed to be careful because, like he had told Macario, he had his own secret. It was one that could change his entire life if anyone ever found out about it. His secrets were one of the reasons why he didn't have many close friends. It was easier to keep people at arm's length than let them in and risk losing everything.

His mother had gone through a tough, lonely life to ensure Tanner had a good future. He wasn't going to dishonor her memory by revealing what she'd worked so hard to conceal.

He wandered into the living room then dropped onto the couch. He wouldn't look at his watch again. Macario wasn't late or anything. Tanner was ready early, and nervous about having the man over. All he really wanted to do was drag Macario to his bed and spend the rest of the night learning every inch of Macario's spectacular body. He wanted to lick and suck until Macario begged for him to fuck him.

Leaning his head back on the cushions, Tanner grinned

up at the ceiling. Was Macario exclusively a top, or would he let Tanner fuck him? As much as Tanner liked to be the one doing the fucking once in a while, he'd be willing to give up his ass as often as needed to get Macario in his bed with him. And didn't that make him a complete slut?

His doorbell rang and he sprang to his feet, nerves crashing through him again. *Shit.* He was an adult and it wasn't really a date. He did want to talk to Macario about the case. He'd noticed a few things that might help with ensuring they got the right guy when they found a suspect.

Another ring from the bell got him moving and he went to the front door. Caution had him checking the peephole before he opened it. Macario stood about three feet back and to the side, like most good law enforcement officers. If greeted by a gun, in that position they were less likely to get hit with the first bullet.

"Thanks for coming over," Tanner said.

Macario stepped inside and took off his cowboy hat. "I'll admit it was the lure of good tequila and food that brought me here."

Why did a shock of disappointment run through Tanner at Macario's words? Just because the man had kissed him last night like he'd wanted Tanner spread eagle and begging on his bed didn't mean Macario was truly interested in him. It could have been the alcohol, and Tanner had had enough alcohol-clouded one-night stands in his life.

"You can hang your hat there." He gestured to the coat tree in the corner of the foyer before strolling back toward the kitchen. "I made enchiladas. Is that okay?"

"Fuck."

The curse was the only warning he got. A strong hand gripped his arm and whirled him around. He stumbled into Macario's embrace, lifting his gaze to stare at the man. Macario dipped his head down, taking Tanner's mouth like an invading army storming a beachhead. Tanner didn't have the mental capacity at that moment to do anything except lift his arms and wrap them around Macario's shoulders.

Their tongues stroked and teased. Macario tasted minty and smelled wonderfully clean, so he must have stopped by his own place to shower and change. Tanner appreciated it, and a little bit of hope blossomed inside him. Not just because of the kiss. If Macario had changed and cleaned up, that could mean he considered this more than just a working meeting. Of course, having his tongue halfway down Tanner's throat might be a more obvious sign.

The oven timer dinged and they broke apart. Tanner fought the urge to press his fingers to his tingling lips. Holy hell, that had to be the hottest kiss he'd ever engaged in. His erection ached and he wished he'd worn sweatpants or something looser than his jeans because he could feel the zipper biting into his hard flesh.

"Well, I don't think I've ever been greeted quite as enthusiastically," he teased.

"Sorry." Macario actually blushed. "All I could think about today was kissing you. It helped after the crappy start to my morning."

He reached out to rub his thumb over Macario's cheek. "I'm not complaining, Macario. I kept trying to tell myself that this was just a working dinner. Didn't quite convince myself because I keep hoping we'll end up naked at some point."

Macario swallowed and nodded. "I'll admit to doing some hoping of my own."

"Come on. Let's eat and talk about the case. After that, we can figure out what we want for dessert."

He led the way into the kitchen. "If you want to grab the salad and drinks, I'll get the enchiladas out of the oven."

"What do you want? Beer or soda?" Macario stuck his head in the refrigerator. "I see you got the limes. Where's the tequila?"

Tanner chuckled. "I'll have a beer for now. The tequila can do along with dessert. We can do body shots."

He hid his smile as Macario choked slightly. After putting on his oven mitts, Tanner slid the pan out and carried it to the table. Macario set the salad and beers down before snagging Tanner as he walked by.

They stared into each other's eyes and Tanner grew uncomfortable. What was Macario searching for as he looked into Tanner's face? If he was looking for something, would he find it? Tanner shifted and Macario let him go.

"You know, this probably isn't a good idea."

Tanner knew what Macario was talking about. "Probably not, but I don't want to wait until this case gets solved. Maybe once my lust is quenched, I can hold out until afterward." He winked, but became serious again. "Don't worry. I'm an adult and I can ensure my private life doesn't mix with my job. I won't attack you in the middle of the Bureau office or anything."

They sat and Tanner dished out the food. Macario took a bite and moaned.

"This is really good, reminds me of the food José made."

"Really? José was a good cook?" Tanner bit back all the other questions he wanted to ask. The set of Macario's shoulders and face told Tanner the man was very private and didn't share personal information freely.

Not that Tanner blamed him. Most people had skeletons in their closets they didn't want to see the light of day. He respected Macario's privacy.

"Only those traditional Mexican dishes. José never really got the hang of cooking American food." Macario laughed softly. "There were times I'd kill for a hamburger and fries."

"I know what you mean. My mother worked a lot, so she didn't have time to make dinner most nights for me. When I was fourteen, she taught me how to cook, but only her favorite dishes that were all Mexican. I eventually learned how to fix other types, yet I tend to fall back on her recipes when I want to impress someone." Tanner bit his bottom lip, wishing he could take that last part back.

"Was your father around?" Macario frowned at his plate like he hadn't meant to ask that question, and was choosing to ignore the 'impress' part of what Tanner had said.

"Not since I was three or four. It was hard at times, but Mama and I helped each other." Tanner sighed. "She died last year."

Macario covered his hand and squeezed. "Sorry to hear that. I lost José about five years ago and there wasn't ever anyone but the two of us."

"We're quite the pair, aren't we?" He lifted their entwined fingers and brushed a kiss over Macario's knuckles. "Let's get all the depressing stuff out of the way. I really want to get back to making out with you."

They let go of each other and by mutual agreement, kept conversation to the minimum while they ate. Once they were finished, they cleaned up and took the bottle of tequila out into the living room where the folders from the case sat on the coffee table. They stared at the manila pile for a moment.

"Okay. I think the ME figured out all the victims were killed by the same knife, giving us the right to assume he has an affinity with knives. He likes to torture them first. Each one has signs of struggling on her wrists and legs. Yet he doesn't rape them, or at least, there are no signs of sexual penetration." Tanner flipped open the top folder and pulled out the wide shot of how the victim was displayed.

Macario rumbled low in his throat, and shooting him a glance, Tanner saw rage simmering in the man's eyes. There was something different about this victim, Tanner knew it, because while there had been a certain urgency in Macario's voice when they'd first met, there hadn't been this deep anger. He made a mental note to push a little harder next time the subject came up.

"Ignoring the victim herself, I studied the way she was displayed in a five-pointed style. When you see something like that, your immediate response is..." He looked at Macario.

The man had turned away from the picture. He fumbled with the tequila bottle's cap and managed to remove it. Tanner sat back and watched as Macario poured himself a shot with shaking hands. Macario was lucky he didn't spill a drop of the liquor. A dash of salt then Macario gulped down the alcohol.

"Your usual response would be…?" Tanner prompted again.

Macario grimaced and set the glass down. "Satan worship. Isn't that usually what that symbol means, if it's a pentagram?"

"Right."

"But you don't believe that." Macario met Tanner's gaze. "What do you think?"

Tanner pursed his lips and stared at the picture for a second. "I think he's messing with us. It might be part of his ritual, but I don't think it's an important aspect of it. I checked all of the photos taken at each scene. The star isn't always complete or perfect. It's almost like he throws it in as an afterthought."

"Like throwing red herrings in to distract us from the important issues?"

"Yes and no. Some of it I believe he's making up as he goes along. He plans out his abductions. He has to be following the women before he grabs them. No witnesses have come forward yet, meaning he knows where to grab them and when to do it. We've identified all five victims, so he doesn't take them from the homeless or the prostitutes. If he did, it would be harder to identify them."

"He's either very arrogant or very stupid."

Tanner walked to the window, looking out over his front yard. "I'm inclined to lean toward the former rather than the later. The sophistication of the kidnapping and killing speaks to a highly ordered mind. Oh, I'm not saying he's a genius or anything like that, but he's not stupid either."

"He's going to kill again, isn't he?"

Bracing his hands against the window frame, Tanner nodded. "I'm afraid there'll be another woman sooner than we expect. He's got a taste for the fear now, and it's a hungry monster."

He heard the clink of glass on glass and turned to spot Macario standing, holding out a shot glass. Tanner stalked to where Macario stood and reached for the saltshaker. He pushed into Macario's personal space, licking a line along the man's neck.

Macario tilted his head, giving Tanner more room. He sprinkled the salt on Macario's wet skin. After taking the glass, he sucked the salt from his soon-to-be lover's neck before slamming back the tequila. They both gasped.

Tanner started to reach for the bottle to pour more out, but Macario shoved him down on the couch. Tanner just barely got his glass on the floor before Macario landed on top of him. He spread his legs as best he could, making room for Macario's hips.

"I decided I'd rather just suck on you."

Tanner's cock stiffened, and he moaned as their groins met. "Fuck me."

"I'll get to that, but first, I think we're wearing too many clothes."

Fumbling, they somehow removed their shirts, and Tanner's eyes closed as Macario lowered his hairy chest down on his. God, he loved a man with chest hair, maybe because he didn't have much of his own. Rearing up, he crushed their mouths together, trying to control the kiss. Macario wouldn't let him.

Macario threaded his fingers through Tanner's hair, holding him still while Macario conquered him. Opening, Tanner let Macario sweep his tongue and he sucked on it. Tequila and jalapeño peppers was a common combination. Tanner thought it just might be his favorite flavor now, especially if it came mixed with Macario's own unique taste.

While Macario made love to his mouth, Tanner slid his hands down Macario's broad back to grip his ass and squeeze. Macario flexed his muscles and Tanner moaned low in his throat. Shit. The man was built and Tanner couldn't wait for Macario to bury his cock in Tanner's ass.

Macario bit Tanner's bottom lip then bathed the pain away. Tanner tipped his head back, closing his eyes as Macario licked a line along his jaw and down to his neck. He whimpered as Macario placed several stinging kisses in a row, ending at his nipple.

"Please," he whispered as Macario breathed warm air over his hard flesh.

Hot moisture surrounded his nipple when Macario wrapped his lips around it. Tanner arched, cradling the back of Macario's head to keep the man right there. Teeth and tongue drove Tanner closer to the edge. He kept his other hand on Macario's butt, and they ground against each other.

Finally, Macario pulled away from him and climbed to his feet. "I'm too old to make out on your couch. Let's move this to the bedroom."

Arguing about that wasn't in Tanner's plan, so he took the hand Macario held out to him and allowed the man to haul him to his feet. They stumbled down the hallway, pausing to kiss and struggle with zippers and belts. By the time they shut the bedroom door behind them, Macario's jeans were open and his cock rose proudly from the fabric.

Tanner dropped to his knees and fisted Macario's cock. "I want to taste this."

Macario pressed against Tanner's shoulders. "Where are your condoms?"

Tanner saw the seriousness in Macario's eyes. He pushed to his feet and made his way to the bathroom. "Get undressed and on the bed. I'll be right back."

He'd forgotten to stock up on lube and rubbers in the nightstand next to the bed. Opening the drawer under the sink, he grabbed the bottle of slick and the entire box of condoms. Not that they were going to use all of them that night, but he liked to be optimistic.

The sight greeting him as he stepped back into his bed froze him in his tracks. Macario lay on the bed, back propped up by pillows. He had one leg bent at the knee and the other angled out to give Tanner a mouth-watering view of his cock and balls. Macario stroked his fat shaft, swiping his palm across the head on each upstroke.

Tanner tossed the lube next to Macario's hip and ripped the box to get a foil packet. He put the box next to the bottle before crawling onto the bed between Macario's legs. He tore open the packet, shoved Macario's hand out of the way then rolled the rubber on.

Without saying anything, he leaned down and swallowed Macario's cock down. He didn't have much gag reflex, so he could take it in until his nose was buried in the curls around the base of Macario's shaft.

"Holy fuck, Tanner." Macario gripped the sides of Tanner's head while he thrust in and out of his mouth.

Tanner let Macario do as he wanted while he made sure he applied hard enough suction and tongue. Saliva dripped down over Macario's balls, tempting Tanner. He fondled Macario's furred balls, squeezing and tugging slightly. Not enough to hurt him, but to add an edge to the sensation. He teased the soft skin behind them, and Macario moaned.

Slipping his fingers into his mouth, Tanner got them as wet as he could before he reached behind to rub over Macario's hole. The man tensed, but didn't pull away from him. Tanner didn't press in, just played with the puckered flesh.

Macario tapped Tanner's shoulder. Not moving away from his position, Tanner glanced up.

"You can do it. I haven't bottomed in a while, but go ahead."

Tanner pulled off and eased up, bracing his hands on either side of Macario's head. "Are you sure? I don't mind bottoming this time."

Macario shrugged. "Fine. You can do me next time."

"Sounds like a plan for me." He grinned down at Macario and picked up the lube. "Why don't you get me ready while I suck on you a little bit more?"

A shudder racked Macario's body and the man nodded.

"Okay. Works for me."

Tanner handed Macario the bottle of lube and turned to straddle Macario, allowing the man access to his ass while he returned his attention to Macario's erection. He placed just the head of Macario's shaft in his mouth and teased it with his tongue.

Macario hissed, but didn't lose focus on what he was supposed to do. Cool slick swiped over Tanner's opening. He sucked in a deep breath and pushed back as Macario breached his ass. Soon they were moving together – Macario shoving up into Tanner's mouth while Tanner rocked back onto Macario's fingers.

The pressure built and the tingling at the base of Tanner's spine warned him that his climax was near. He rolled over and onto his back and grabbed his legs behind his knees, bringing them back to expose himself.

"Fuck me now, Macario. I don't want to come until you're in me."

Macario settled between Tanner's thighs like he belonged there then positioned the head of his cock at Tanner's hole and eased in, inch by inch. Tanner bit his lip, wanting to yell at the man to shove the full length in as fast as possible.

He stared up at Macario, saw the gritted teeth, and knew Macario was trying not to hurt him. He reached up and caressed Macario's chin.

"Slam into me, Macario. I can take it. I want you hard and fast. We can do it slow later."

Macario met his gaze and whatever the man saw in Tanner's eyes convinced him.

"Brace yourself."

Putting his hands against the headboard, Tanner nodded, and Macario drove a shout from him. Their lovemaking became primitive and almost violent. Macario held Tanner's hip with one hand while bending over him and reaming Tanner's ass.

"That's it. Right there." Tanner grunted as Macario managed to nail his gland.

Whatever smooth rhythm Macario had started with disappeared as he drove closer and closer to the cliff. Tanner tightened his inner muscles, drawing Macario's climax from him. Macario thrust into him and froze, head thrown back and a yell filled the room. With a tug or two at his own cock, Tanner came as well, his cum spilling out over his stomach. Macario collapsed and Tanner gasped as he caught all of Macario's weight.

"Sorry. As soon as I can remember how to move, I'll get off you and clean up."

Tanner chuckled softly. "It's okay. We have time."

He ran his fingers through Macario's sweaty hair while their breathing eased. After a few minutes, Macario slipped out of him, eliciting a quiet whimper from Tanner. He stared up at the ceiling while Macario headed toward the bathroom. Tanner heard water running and turned when he heard Macario come back into the room. His lover washed him off before tossing the cloth in the direction of the other room.

They settled under the covers. Would Macario want to cuddle or would he simply fall asleep like a lot of Tanner's lovers had? Tanner liked to snuggle after sex. It helped make him feel less alone. He bit back his sigh of relief when Macario maneuvered their bodies around so Tanner's back rested against Macario's chest. His strong arms lay over Tanner's waist to curl over Tanner's heart.

"Let's sleep for a bit, then maybe you can fuck me," Macario mumbled.

Tanner didn't answer, just patted Macario's hand in agreement. He let his eyes drift closed and fell asleep, surrounded by Macario's heat.

* * * *

A noise woke Tanner later that night. Waking up on his back, he reached out to touch the mattress next to him. No one was there. Had Macario woken up and left? Maybe after getting his rocks off, Macario had decided there wasn't any point in doing it again. Was it the front door closing he'd heard?

Another noise caught his attention and he climbed out of bed. He dug out a pair of sweats and his back-up gun from the dresser. Opening the bedroom door, he stood, listening to see if he could figure out where the person was in his house.

Clinking of glass drew him to the living room and he entered to see Macario pour some tequila.

"Isn't it a little late for drinking?"

Macario must have known Tanner was there because he didn't react when Tanner spoke. "It's not too late for drinking when you can't sleep."

Tanner sat on the couch, watching Macario stare out of the bow window. Tension was evident in the set of the man's shoulders. What was he worried about?

"Obviously our sleeping together shouldn't have happened now. We're working on a case together and our focus should be on finding the killer."

Turning to look at him, Macario nodded. "You're right, but I don't regret what we did."

"Neither do I and I hope we do it again. Several times, but maybe after the case's solved."

Macario snorted. "I doubt I'm going to be able to wait that long."

And why did that statement make Tanner proud? He pushed the thought away to look at later. He noticed how Macario had the folder for the last knife victim open and the photos scattered across the coffee table.

"Who was she, Macario? I can tell you knew the latest victim."

Macario stared down at his drink. "How'd you guess?"

Tanner fiddled with the edge of one of the photos. "I'm trained to be observant. I noticed your reaction when you saw something on her body."

"A birthmark inside her left elbow," Macario muttered.

"Who was she?"

Macario slammed back his tequila before saying, "You already know her name. Marissa Levisten. When I was fifteen, she was my foster sister for six months."

"Were you both part of the system?"

Tanner could tell Macario hated baring his private life to a man who was practically a stranger, even if they'd just had sex together. Tanner didn't push. He'd take whatever Macario would give him for now.

"I was. The state took me away from my crack-whore mother and shuffled me from family to family. I landed at the Levistens for six months until Mr. Levisten transferred out of state. I lost track of them after that."

"How did you get back in touch with her?"

"It was only in the last couple of months or so that I found out she and her family lived in Houston. We talked at least once a week, but I wouldn't really say we were close. We were just starting to rebuild our friendship."

Tanner nodded and stayed silent for a moment while Macario poured another tequila.

"Why not tell your boss you knew her? Your number is bound to come up on her phone records."

"I've made the decision to tell Billingsley in the morning. I informed her parents earlier today and promised them I'd find her killer."

"I get that, but you're going to have to do some fancy talking not to get taken off this case." Tanner stood and strolled to where Macario leaned against the window frame. He rested his hand on Macario's shoulder. "I'll do everything I can to keep you working with me."

"I appreciate it."

Tanner took the glass from Macario's hand and entwined their fingers. He set the glass down on the end table as they passed it, heading back to the bedroom.

"Time to sleep. You're going to run yourself into the ground and that won't help the Levistens get closure." Tanner pointed to the bed. "Lie down. I'll set the alarm so you can get up early enough to go home and change before you go in."

Macario didn't argue and climbed into bed. Tanner retrieved two aspirins and a glass of water for his lover.

"Here. Take these. It'll help with the headache you're going to have in the morning."

Again Macario didn't say anything, and Tanner wondered if the man regretted telling Tanner all that he had. Tanner didn't care. He wouldn't break the trust Macario had shown him by allowing him to see into his personal life. Eventually, maybe Tanner would show the same trust and tell Macario about the skeletons in his closet.

Joining Macario in bed, Tanner embraced him and Macario sighed, relaxing into Tanner's arms.

"Sleep. The case isn't going anywhere. We'll look at everything again tomorrow."

Macario grunted, and Tanner smiled in the darkness. Not much of a talker late at night. Tanner would have to remember that.

His phone beeped and he managed to snatch it from the stand without waking Macario. Flipping it open, he read the message.

Leaving Houston. B gone for a week or so.

K. B careful, he texted back.

Boss says u b careful as well. Doesn't want to have to kill anyone.

Tanner snorted softly, but accepted the fact that if he ever did get hurt, the person who hurt him would probably be dead before the sun rose the next day.

I'll b fine. Have a good trip.

He tossed the phone off the bed, not caring where it landed. Wiggling a little, he slipped further down under the covers and closed his eyes. Yes, morning would be there quickly, and he needed to get some rest to help Macario find the guy who'd killed his foster sister.

Chapter Four

Tanner stood in his office, arms folded, staring at the pictures taped to the large dry-erase board attached to one wall. With just a quick once-over, he knew the same man killed the women. The savageness of the knife wounds and the way each woman was displayed spoke of a deep-seated anger toward females. Yet the precision of the cuts told Tanner the killer was comfortable with a knife and knew how to use the blade to cause maximum pain or torture.

The man favored a large blade with no serrations, like a Ka-Bar or combat knife. Tanner made a note to double-check the ME's report on the actual wounds. Also, he'd have to dig through the crime scene photos again to see if they had any close-up pictures of them. Even they could give him some more clues to the killer's identity.

Frowning, he shuffled the photos, pulling out the close-up images of each victim's breast. He taped them to the board under their names and next to the images of the entire body. There was something in the design carved into the flesh. He could almost make it out, but the intricate swirls hid whatever was there perfectly.

Tanner grabbed his phone and dialed Macario's number.

"Guzman."

"Hey, Macario, it's Tanner."

"Hey. How's it going?"

A slight hesitation marred Macario's question, and Tanner smiled. Apparently Macario worried Tanner was going to become clingy or talk about what they'd done the night before. He didn't have to worry. Tanner wasn't going to say anything. It was one night and nothing more could be done until the case was over. Starting any kind of relationship in the middle of a case was difficult enough, but when one of the investigating officers was related to one of the victims, the difficulty level went even higher.

"Good. Do you have the original photos of all the crime scenes on your computer?"

Macario grunted and Tanner heard typing in the background. "Yeah. Why?"

"Can you email them to me? I need to enlarge some of them."

"Sure. Do you have something?" Macario sounded cautiously optimistic.

No cop worth his weight in experience would get excited about any clue, except the one leading to the capture of the killer.

Tanner shrugged, even though he knew Macario couldn't see him. "Maybe. There's a symbol or something entwined in the swirls the bastard carves into their left breast. I can't make it out with the pictures I have. I thought I'd enlarge them and see if that helps."

"You doing it yourself?" Macario asked.

Tanner sat at his desk and brought up his email. "Yeah. I learned how to do all that stuff when I realized usually the techs don't work at three in the morning when I get a good idea and need to see something. It's not that hard."

"Probably wouldn't be for someone who can use a computer without breaking it," the Texas Ranger mumbled.

"Not very computer literate, huh?" Tanner's fingers flew over his keyboard.

Macario chuckled. "I do all right. As long as I can email and type up my reports, I'm happy."

"Yeah, most people don't need much more than that."

A new message appeared from Macario and Tanner opened it to start downloading the file.

"Thanks. I'll let you get back to what you were doing."

"We're trying to retrace the days before each victim disappeared. I'm trying to see what connects them because there has to be some reason why he chose those particular women."

Tanner snorted softly. "They always have a reason for picking them. Doesn't mean we'll ever know what it is."

"That's the frustrating thing."

"We'll just have to ask when we catch him." Tanner's computer dinged when the file was done. He opened it to make sure everything worked. "Thanks for sending the pictures, Macario. I'm going to start working on them. I'll call you if I get anything."

"You know how to get a hold of me." Macario paused for a few seconds before continuing, "Do you want to get together tonight and talk over what we've done for the day?"

Tanner's body tensed as he imagined what they could end up talking about, but he didn't automatically assume Macario would want more sex. He wasn't going to make a big deal of it one way or another.

"Sure. You want to call me when you're ready for dinner? I'll be working on this case as much as possible all day, though I do have a couple others that I have to go over as well. I'll meet you wherever you want." Tanner wandered over to the board, staring at the pictures. "But we should probably call a meeting of the task force, so I can tell them what I figured out so far. Also, you can compare my beginning profile with what your profiler did."

"You still haven't read the report?"

"No. I don't want to prejudice my thoughts. You and Billingsley wanted a second set of eyes looking at this. That's what I'm giving you without being compromised by any other opinion. Once my report is done, we'll go through both profiles and combine them to ensure we don't miss something important by either of us."

"Okay. I'll call when I've got the meeting set up. We're still on for dinner though." Macario hung up.

Tanner set his phone down, then settled back at his desk, opening the software to enlarge the particular part of the pictures interesting him. He printed multiple copies of them before taping one print to each collection of photographs on the board. The other set he carried to a chair he placed next to the window in his office. He'd grabbed a magnifying glass out of his desk as he went by.

Why did the carving intrigue him so much? All of his instincts told him it held the secret to the killer's identity, even though he could already tell something about the man from the photographs. He'd written down some of his thoughts and would type up a preliminary report for Sam and Major Billingsley including everything he'd told Macario the night before.

The display of the women was just a red herring in a way. Tanner was sure of it. Yes, like he said to Macario, it was part of the man's ritual, but only as a way to disguise another part of it that meant more to him. Tanner scrubbed his chin and squinted out of the window.

Damn! He was going to have to go through all the evidence collected at the scenes. He hated touching items connected to such violent murders. At times, it felt like the pain and terror of the victims rubbed off on him. After particularly horrific cases, he would take a vacation to the islands or even up into the Rockies, trying to erase from his psyche all the hatred and insanity.

He understood he wouldn't be able to profile much longer. He didn't have the right mind-set to do it for the rest of his life. Too much violence and death marked a man deep inside, even when he was only responsible for cleaning up the aftermath. He was starting to wish he worked somewhere that prevented the violence, or tried to stop it before it got as far as someone dying.

His desk phone rang and he went to answer it. "Wallace."

"Our meeting is in an hour at your office. You want me to bring anything?"

He smiled at Macario's brisk question. "No. I'll be ready. See you in an hour then."

"See you then."

Macario hung up and Tanner shook his head. The man didn't seem big on conversation and it didn't upset Tanner. He'd learned long ago to entertain himself because it had just been him and his mom while he was growing up. His mom hadn't ever encouraged him to have many friends. He understood her reasoning, but he'd been lonely as a child until he'd learned why they had to keep to themselves.

Tanner had never once questioned his mother's choices for their lives. He hardly missed his father once the man was out of the picture. Of course, Tanner's dad had never had much to do with him. He was too busy with his business, so Tanner had always hung out with his mother, and when they'd moved to the States, he'd accepted his new home. He did, however, miss his older brother. Tanner'd been a toddler when his parents divorced, but he did remember how protective his brother had been and how much fun they'd had together.

After opening the top left drawer of his desk, he pulled out a framed picture. He sat down then leaned back in his chair, staring at the photo. It had been taken when he'd graduated from college. His mother had been so proud of him and he'd been excited. As far as Tanner knew, he was the first of his family to graduate from high school, much less college. Once he'd gotten a job with the FBI, he'd been able to help his mother out with bills. She'd only stopped working when she was diagnosed with cancer.

He took after her in his lean build and dark eyes. Until she'd gotten sick, she'd looked more like his older sister than his mother, and she'd always joked about that with him. The months before she'd died were some of the most difficult he'd gone through because he'd been alone with his grief. She hadn't let him dwell on it. She'd kept him laughing, though she had admitted she regretted not being able to see him settled down and in love.

Coming out to his mother had turned out to be easier than he'd expected. She'd cried when he'd told her and he'd thought it was because he'd disappointed her. She'd held his face and smiled up at him, explaining in her heavily accented English that he could never disappoint her. She'd cried because it would be a tough journey he'd undertaken and since she believed God didn't make mistakes, she knew he didn't have a choice.

One of the things she'd hated most about dying was not seeing any grandchildren, even though he'd explained he wouldn't have any. She'd pointed out that many gay couples adopted—it was something they'd often argued about while she had her chemo.

He rubbed his thumb over the glass and murmured, "I miss you, Mama."

A knock on his door caused him to return the picture to the drawer before he called out, "Come in."

MacLaughlin peered around the doorframe. "The Rangers will be here in a few. I wanted to check and make sure you were ready for this."

"Yeah. I'll have a preliminary report ready for everyone. Got some ideas that might be helpful and I'm checking a few other things out as well. I'm going to have to go over to the Rangers' headquarters and look through all the actual evidence from the different crime scenes." Tanner stood and strolled over to the board. He tapped the picture of the first victim. "I think we're missing something."

"Well, don't tell me. Wait until we're all in the same room before you go into your spiel." MacLaughlin shook his head. "I read the Rangers' profile and even if they're only half right, this is one sick fuck."

"They're all sick fucks, boss." Tanner ran his hand over his hair.

"True. How long have you been doing this, Wallace? Six or seven years?"

"Seven."

Probably six years too many. His head pounding, he wandered back to his desk to dig out a bottle of aspirin. Shaking out four pills, he dry-swallowed them with a grimace.

"You would think you'd get used to this after a while, but I've been in the Bureau for almost twenty years, and I still haven't gotten used to the horrible shit humans do to each other." MacLaughlin frowned. "Of course, I don't get too in-depth in the cases anymore, not like you."

Tanner wished he didn't have to study photos like the ones in front of him, but he did, and those mutilated bodies haunted his dreams at night. When he'd first started in the Behavioral Science Unit, he'd drank himself to sleep every night, trying to drown out the blood and gore. But all the alcohol and the coffee he'd drunk had gotten him was a pounding headache the next morning, and an ulcer. Finally, he'd simply learned to compartmentalize every aspect of his life. He did his best to leave his work at the office, but it didn't always happen. The victims of this latest killer would be one of those cases where he would see their faces in his dreams.

"I'll let you get back to the case. I'll see you in about thirty minutes. We'll just meet in here since you have the board set up." MacLaughlin waved a hand to the pictures.

"I'll be ready."

After his boss had left, Tanner went through the bullpen, nodding to some of his fellow agents as he headed toward the break room. While he waited for his water to heat, he grabbed a napkin and tried to draw the carvings. He took his tea and the drawings back into his office. He sat at his desk and closed his eyes, continuing to draw them as he could remember them.

"I didn't realize the Bureau agreed to afternoon naps. Maybe I should come work with you."

Tanner flipped Macario off, but didn't open his eyes right away. He heard the chairs scrape on the floor and two grunts as Macario and Billingsley, Tanner assumed, sat. Rustling papers were the only noises for a moment before someone cleared his throat.

"Are you done meditating or whatever the hell you're doing?"

He opened his eyes and rolled them at Macario. "I wasn't meditating, or sleeping for that matter."

Billingsley frowned. "Then what were you doing?"

After pushing the pile of drawings toward Macario and Billingsley, he stood and strolled over to the board. "I've been trying to figure out what symbol is etched into their breasts. It's been hidden by the intricate design, but it's there. I was trying to draw the designs to see if I can repeat it."

MacLaughlin walked in then shook Billingsley's hand. "Good to see you again, Major. Is this everyone?"

"Yes. I'll have Macario update everyone else at headquarters for now. When Agent Wallace has more, we'll call a meeting of the entire task force for him to bring everyone up to speed." Billingsley glanced over at Tanner. "Well, are you ready to wow me, Agent Wallace?"

"I'm not sure what you're expecting, Major. What I tell you will probably be what your own profiler already found out during his examination of the scenes."

"Maybe, or maybe you'll have seen something he missed. I'd rather catch this asshole than worry about the feelings of the men working for me." Billingsley shrugged. "You might be right as well. You might not see anything new, but you've only been looking for a couple days. I'll give you the benefit of the doubt."

"Thank you."

Macario stared at Tanner's drawings like he was trying to see what Tanner was talking about. Whether Macario believed him or not, Tanner didn't care. His instincts screamed to him that if he just looked beneath the surface, he could find clues to the killer's identity.

"The floor is yours, Tanner." MacLaughlin gestured toward him.

Tanner folded his arms over his chest and turned to look at the three men seated in the room. "I've gone over the pictures several times, looked at them from all the different angles available. I can tell you some basic things about the guy."

He pointed to the photos, tracing the wounds with his finger. "You're definitely looking for a male. Not just because a majority of serial killers are male. If the killer was female, she would have to be extremely strong, and if a female bodybuilder was in the area, someone would have noticed."

Macario snorted. "That's true. There haven't been any witnesses come forward. They only seem to notice the women were missing, but they don't know who took them."

Tanner nodded. "I'm not surprised. Okay, so you're looking for a male, probably around six-four or five, and he's strong. None of the blood tests came back positive for drugs, which leads me to believe he overpowered them before stuffing them in his car or however he transports them. More than likely, he drives a van or a truck with a cap on the back, so he can move them without anyone seeing."

"Do you have a thought about race or age?" Macario pulled out a notebook and pen.

"He'll be in his mid-to-late thirties. As for race, I'm not sure. I haven't seen any indicators to make you focus on one ethic group over another, though traditional African-Americans don't tend to be serial killers." Tanner gestured again to the knife injuries. "Another thing suggested by the wounds is he'll be left handed."

"Okay, explain why you believe that," MacLaughlin spoke up. "I've never understood how you profilers come up with that from just looking at the wounds."

"Macario, could you pull out the ME's autopsy reports for the first four victims from their files on my desk?" Tanner nodded toward the pile of folders. "We don't have the papers for the latest one, but I'm confident they'll tell us the same things as the others."

Macario grimaced at the mention of Marissa, but dug through all the files to pull out the right reports. He started to hand them to Tanner, but Tanner shook his head.

"I don't know if you all want to look at them, but the ME

was very thorough. He measured the depth of each stab wound. His determinations helped me with my ultimate conclusions. When you have a left-handed attacker striking from the front, the wounds will be deeper on the right side of the victim, even if the person being attacked wasn't fighting back. Again, based on the evidence found at the scenes, we're operating on the assumption that he bound them."

"But wouldn't the depth of the wounds be the same on both sides if there wasn't any struggling or fight?" Billingsley asked, reading through one of the ME's reports.

"Not entirely. You would still have deeper wounds on the right side, simply because the strength of the dominate hand would bring more force into his strikes." He shrugged. "It's not an exact science, but I haven't been wrong yet when I've used the theory."

He picked his tea from his desk and took a sip, wrinkling his nose in distaste because it was cold. There wasn't time to get more. He strolled back over to the board and stared at the pictures for a moment.

"The perp hangs his victim by her wrists before he starts the torture," Tanner commented softly as his gaze outlined the bruises on the delicate wrists. "He doesn't kill them where he dumps them, but he uses the same type of room or spot. Industrial warehouse with brick walls."

MacLaughlin started to say something, but Tanner saw Macario stop him with a quick shake of his head. Sometimes profiling was almost like being psychic, yet Tanner's knowledge came from studying hundreds, if not thousands of crime scene photos. He read articles and interviewed mass murderers, serial killers and sociopaths. Each piece of research etched a scar into his soul until sometimes at night, Tanner stared at the ceiling and wondered how much more of this he could do before he went over the edge into darkness himself.

"If you look at the photographs of their backs, you can see where their skin scraped against the brick each time he struck them. I'm sure the ME did tests to see if he could get any residue out of those abrasions."

"Did you read any of the ME's reports?" Macario sounded surprised at the possibility.

"Only the parts about the knife wounds. I haven't gotten to the non-fatal injuries yet." He stepped over to the second victim. "He starts with a shallow cut or two, teasing them with the hope that all he wants is to rape them. The perp likes the power he garners from playing with them. It's not about sex and he wouldn't degrade himself by touching them in that way. With each new slice, he goes a little deeper, and as the blood runs down her body, she realizes she's not getting out. That's when she starts struggling."

Blinking, he turned to look at the trio of men sitting there. Billingsley and Macario stared at him, a little stunned by Tanner's recitation of what probably happened during the murders. MacLaughlin didn't even blink, since he'd seen Tanner work before.

"What else?" He waved at Tanner to continue.

"He cuts until she passes out from blood loss. Once she's no longer conscious, he slices her throat and leaves her hanging until she bleeds out. After that, he waits until it's safe to move her. At the dump site, he arranges her in the pentagram display." Tanner rubbed his chin. "I'm sure most of the investigators would believe it would have something to do with Satanism, but I don't think that's it. He's messing with us."

"Messing with us? What do you mean?" Billingsley glared at him. "Why would he do that?"

"I mean that the pentagram display is merely something he does as an afterthought. Almost like he's tossing out red herrings for us. It is part of his ritual, but if you notice, it's not always complete or done the same way. If it was an integral part of his ritual, it would the same every time."

Tanner shoved his hands through his hair, tugging on the ends once before he whirled and grabbed the enlarged prints of the carvings. He handed them to the trio.

"I've been studying these all day. I've tried to draw them, which is what I was doing when you arrived. There's something inside the design and I think that's the most important item at the crime scene. Also, I want to go through all the evidence collected at each scene. It might help me give you more of what to look for in a suspect."

He went to the window and stared out at the people strolling on the sidewalk below. Most of them were aware of the killer stalking Houston's streets, but none of them believed they could be victims. As of that moment, every woman in the city could be his next prey.

"Have we figured out how he chooses them?" Billingsley glanced over at Macario.

"Not yet." Macario growled low in his throat, frustration evident in the sound.

"We know he must follow them for some time before he takes them," Tanner interjected. "The patterns of the crime scenes and the actual process of the killing speaks of an organized mind. Our killer doesn't do this on a whim."

Macario met his gaze with a raised eyebrow and he smiled.

"I'm sure the investigators will come up with the connecting piece between the women before too long. Unfortunately, I must admit I don't think it'll be soon enough to save our next victim. He's already stalking her and will probably take her within the next two days or so."

"God damn!" Billingsley shot to his feet. "We've got to get something on this man before we have mass panic and the women start carrying guns. We could have innocent men being shot for nothing more than being in the wrong place at the wrong time."

Tanner understood the major's anger and worry, but he also knew there was no way, without some kind of miracle, for them to get the identity of the killer before he took the next woman. It wasn't optimal, but it was the realistic outlook, though Tanner would have preferred the miracle.

"We will. You just have to give your men and mine time.

Very few of these types of cases go unsolved. Something will pop up and our guy will make a mistake. Trust me, our men are the best at their jobs." Tanner watched as the major stalked around the room.

"How many more are going to die before we get him?" Billingsley paced Tanner's office, dodging the other men and the furniture.

Tanner shrugged. "It's hard to say. He's gotten a true taste for this and his need is growing. He killed one a month for four months, but the fifth only came two weeks after the last one. That's why we'll have another victim here soon. He's escalating and until we can get a witness or some other break in the case, we'll have more deaths."

"Fuck!" Billingsley rubbed the back of his neck and sighed. "I know it's not your fault, Mac, or yours either, Wallace. It just drives me crazy to know that sick fuck walks the streets of Houston and gets off killing women."

"We're with you, James." MacLaughlin stood and clapped Billingsley on the shoulder while glancing over at Tanner and Macario. "We should leave and let them discuss things. I don't know about you, but I have some other cases I need to look over."

"You're right. Mac, I'll expect you in my office first thing tomorrow with an update."

"Yes, sir." Macario didn't look too upset about pulling an all-nighter.

Of course, he'd probably pulled quite a few since the murders had started happening.

"Tanner, you'll work directly with Guzman until the case is solved."

Tanner nodded. "Yes, sir."

Macario and Tanner watched their bosses leave. After the door shut behind them, they looked at each other.

"Guess we're having a working dinner tonight."

"I'm pretty used to those. I tend to take my work home with me." Tanner gestured to the pile of folders on his desk. He checked his watch. "It's close to five. Why don't we grab some take out and head over to my place? We can work from there."

"I'll meet you there in an hour. What do you want for dinner?" Macario grabbed his hat from where he'd hung it on Tanner's coat tree in the corner.

"Surprise me. I'm not very picky when it comes to food. Oh, except for mac 'n' cheese. Ate too much of it growing up because it was cheap and easy to make. At times, it was the only thing Mama could afford." Tanner started to gather up all the files and copies of the photos. "If you hang on a minute, I'll walk out with you."

As they left the office, he stopped by to let MacLaughlin know he was working from home the rest of the night. His boss didn't care where Tanner worked as long as the files were secure and the work got done. Macario tipped his hat toward Tanner when they parted in the parking garage.

Tanner put his briefcase on the floor of the passenger seat before walking over to his side of the car. After sliding behind the wheel, he rested his head back against the seat and breathed deep. *Christ!* It was going to be hard to focus on the case with Macario in the same room with him, especially after having tasted the man the night before. Yet he could be professional when he needed to be and the case came first, no matter what Tanner's body demanded.

Chapter Five

He watched as she strolled down the sidewalk, window-shopping like women seemed to enjoy doing. He never understood that urge, but hell, he'd never understood a woman yet. He checked his watch as she ducked into one of the shops. Yes, it was time for her daily cup of caramel frappuccino. He'd followed her into the coffee shop one day, simply to see if she noticed him.

The woman had smiled at him, but she'd never once acted like she'd noticed him following her and that was important. To achieve his goal, she couldn't know he stalked her. He lounged on a bench just down the street from where she got her coffee. He opened the newspaper he'd bought earlier and read the article about the Knife Killer. A smirk crossed his face as he read the shit the reporter had written about him.

The police knew nothing about him, though reading how the Rangers were taking over the murder cases from HPD and were consulting with the FBI did cause him to hesitate for a moment. Then he shook his worry off. It didn't matter. They could get a psychic to work the case and he would still out-think them.

He peered over the edge of the paper as she walked past him. With long blonde hair and big blue eyes, she looked good, if he went for that kind of woman. He didn't, but he understood why the other guys on the sidewalk watched her stroll past, her hips swinging.

Her phone rang and she dug it out from her purse. Once standing, he folded the newspaper and tucked it under his arm. He straightened his suit coat before heading after her, acting like a businessman on his way home from work. Slowly weaving his way through the crowd, he came up just behind her. She chatted on the phone, ignoring everyone around her. Hell, he could pick her pocket without the woman realizing it until she got home.

Shaking his head, he eased back, not ready to make his move yet. The urgency wasn't as big as he needed it to be to take her. It was still running on the satisfaction from his last kill. The woman had been a fighter. It had taken longer for her to stop struggling and lose consciousness than the other women. There had been far more slices on her than he liked. It had looked messy when he'd finished laying her out in the pentagram.

He trailed her to the corner of her street. He knew what she was going to do. She would head home and change before heading out to the gym for her nightly workout. Once finished with that, she'd return home and stay in during the week. On the weekends, she'd work out, go home, change then head out to one of the clubs. He'd followed her while she'd gone dancing with friends and on a date. He'd been tracing her routine for a week or more, even before he'd taken the last woman, he'd been searching for his next victim.

Continuing on past her corner, he went down to the next one and dropped the act, moving quickly toward where he'd left his truck. He would come back in a day or two after finding the perfect place to take her.

* * * *

Macario held the bag of BBQ food in his hand as he knocked on Tanner's door. He glanced around at the small front porch and yard. It was well-kept, but the railings needed a coat of paint.

Tanner opened the door and Macario caught his breath at the welcoming smile on Tanner's face. He didn't remember anyone ever looking as happy to see him as Tanner looked, not even his adopted father. He held up the bag of food. "BBQ."

"Oh good, and you got it from Goode's."

"Where else would I get it from?" He grinned as he walked inside.

Laughing, Tanner led the way to the kitchen. "True. I'll grab the plates, if you want to unpack the food. What do you want to drink?"

"Beer."

Macario set the food on the table while Tanner set out the plates and silverware. He grabbed some paper towels and sat across from Tanner. They split the ribs and brisket between them, along with the corn bread and baked beans. Silence reigned except for an occasional moan of pleasure for the food.

With the last rib finished, Macario leaned back in his chair and groaned. "I always end up working out twice as long after eating at Goode's."

"It's definitely a meal where you can feel your cholesterol climbing with each bite." Tanner pushed away from the table and grimaced as he stood. "All I want to do right now is curl up on my couch and take a nap."

Macario chuckled. "Sounds good to me, but we do need to do some work tonight."

"I know."

Tanner started to clear the table and Macario stood to help him. They got the dishwasher filled and ready quickly. Macario grabbed two more beers out of the refrigerator while Tanner turned the laptop on. He set the bottles down and turned, reaching out to rest his hands on Tanner's hips.

"Before we get into the photos and all that other shit, I need to kiss you."

He could see his declaration had surprised Tanner slightly by the widening of the man's eyes. Yet there wasn't any protest as he pulled Tanner closed to him and brought their lips together. He tasted the tang of the BBQ sauce mixed with the hops from Tanner's beer. He slid his hands around to grip Tanner's ass and deepened the kiss, sweeping his tongue in to tease and duel with Tanner's.

Tanner cradled the back of Macario's head and caressed the skin at the nape of his neck. Matching moans filled the air as they pressed their groins together. *Shit!* All he'd thought about the entire day was how tight Tanner's ass had been around his cock, and those thoughts appeared at the most inappropriate times. Luckily, he'd been sitting at his desk most of the day, but Sorensterm had thought he'd had too much caffeine, considering how much shifting and wiggling he'd done.

Easing back, he rested his forehead against Tanner's and breathed. "You're like a drug I'm becoming addicted to totally by accident."

"I know." Tanner rubbed his thumb over Macario's bottom lip. With a sigh, Tanner stepped away. "We do need to do some work."

After sitting on the couch, Macario glared at the folders on Tanner's coffee table. "I'm not looking forward to this. I've gone through these files so many times I think I have them memorized. I'm not sure looking at everything again will make any difference."

"It can't hurt." Tanner joined him and bumped their shoulders together. "There has to be a connection between them. We just haven't found it yet."

"Of course there is. We have to figure out why he picks the girls he does. What is it about them he wants to kill? Is it really them, or what they represent, that he's killing?"

Tanner grabbed Marissa's file and leaned back against the cushions. "I've been working on that. To be honest, I haven't quite figured out why he kills them the way he does, aside from the fact he likes knives and is most comfortable with them."

Macario frowned. "Does he need another reason than that? I would think slicing a woman until she bleeds is usually done because her killer wants her to suffer a rather painful death."

"If this was a crime of passion and just one victim, I'd say yes. Our perp wants the woman to be frightened and struggle. But there are five victims and nothing I've seen of the crime scenes says this is a crime of passion. He coldly stalks them and takes them without any fear of getting caught. That means he knows what he's doing." Tanner snatched up a pencil and a pad of paper. "I think I'll search the database to see if there are any unsolved crimes fitting this pattern."

"We already did that when we realized we had a serial killer on our hands. Nothing came up but some drug-related killings. We're pretty sure none of these women were involved in drugs or had anything to do with that business." Macario steeled himself and picked up Linda Happleston's file—the first victim. "I wish they were all blondes, or all Hispanic, or something like that. Some obvious connection. I hate when they get sneaky."

Tanner snorted. "There is a connection between them, and you'll find it, Macario. You don't have all the information on the women yet, so there's still stuff out there you don't know about them."

"I feel like each one of these ladies was a good friend," Macario muttered.

"And the deeper you dig into their lives, the more intrusive it feels, yet I'm sure they wouldn't mind as long as it caught their killer in the end." Tanner paused for a second, his head tilted like he just thought of something. "Did you say the only murders you found in the database resembling these were drug-related?"

"Yeah. There were one or two in Texas. A couple in Arizona, and a few in California." Macario dug through the files, trying to remember which one he'd had open when he'd got the information. "Here."

He tugged Amy Bradley's file out. She was the third victim and the one that had clued them into the fact they had a serial killer wandering the streets of Houston. Tanner took it from him.

"I wrote the case numbers down and stuck it in her file. Do you think there might be a connection we just haven't found yet?"

"Hmmm…" Tanner flipped the folder open and shuffled through the papers to pull the right one out.

Macario watched his lover stand and stroll over to the laptop set up on the desk in the corner of the living room. He shrugged when Tanner didn't answer him. He didn't think any of the women were druggies or mules used by the drug cartels to move product. None of them had boyfriends connected to the trade. Every one of the victims seemed perfectly ordinary. None of them engaged in activities putting them in danger, unless one counted going to the clubs of Houston dangerous. Knowing what he knew about what went on in those clubs, Macario would consider them dangerous for women.

He pulled out Linda's credit card statements. He hadn't made it through all of them yet. Linda was a shopper and had a lot of cards to various stores around the city. His head pounded at just the thought of having to stare at all those numbers and try to figure out each small thing that could be used to connect her to the other women.

There was a Post-it note stuck on the last page. After reading it, he double-checked the charge to Tim's Gym. Something jogged his memory and he scrambled to dig out the statements from all the other victims. He swore softly when he realized they didn't have Marissa's statements yet.

"Hey, did you ever get a copy of Marissa's credit card statements?" He glanced over at Tanner.

"Not yet. I asked about them earlier today, but the detective I talked with said they hadn't arrived." Tanner typed, his fingers flying over the keyboard. "You might want to check your email. They might have come in this afternoon while you were gone."

"Good idea. I have to go out and get my briefcase from the car."

Tanner grunted, intent on whatever he was looking at on

his screen. Macario smiled as he left the house and walked to his car. At least Tanner's dedication to his job gave Macario hope they'd catch the bastard sooner rather than later, though knowing there would be another killing soon made his stomach clench.

He popped his trunk and bent to grab his briefcase. Out of the corner of his eye, Macario spotted a dark Suburban parked on the opposite side of the street several houses down from Tanner's. Nothing about the vehicle screamed suspicious, yet Macario's cop instincts pinged on the SUV. He couldn't tell if anyone was in the vehicle because the windows were tinted black.

The angle he stood at didn't give him a good look at the license plate. Frowning, Macario considered going up to the vehicle, but if there was some kind of stakeout happening in the neighborhood, he didn't want to interrupt it. With a shrug, he headed back inside.

"Hey, Tanner, have you seen a black Suburban parked on your street before?"

Tanner glanced up at him and nodded. "A few times. Tinted windows and making all your cop vibes go off?"

"Yeah." Macario set his briefcase on the dining table then opened it before pulling out his laptop. "Does it belong to someone in the neighborhood or is something going down around here?"

"I think it belongs to someone who visits one of the neighborhood teenagers. I keep an eye on it and everything, but so far nothing bad's happened in the area." Tanner waved a hand in the general direction of the kitchen. "I have the license number written down just in case. I ran it and nothing came up."

"I should have known you would be on top of it." Macario booted up his computer and carried it over to the coffee table.

"Why did you want to know about the credit card statements? Do you think you might have something?" Tanner stretched.

The small patch of tanned skin revealed by the lifting of Tanner's shirt distracted Macario for a second. When it disappeared under fabric, he reminded himself of Tanner's question.

"I might, or at least one of the detectives who's been going through the statements might. So far two of our victims have charged something at Tim's Gym. I'm hoping the others will as well."

"It's a start. Could be where he's finding them, but I'm still struggling to figure out how he picks them." Tanner took a copy of the headshot from each file and spread them on the table. He stood there, studying them again. "It's there, just at the edge of my mind, but I can't grasp it. Usually finding the underlying connection is as easy as looking at them. Not this group—all different heights, weights, hair color and eye color. Nothing is the same on each of them."

Macario watched Tanner tug on his bottom lip and bit his own to keep his needy groan from bursting free. They still had more work to do before he could take Tanner to bed. He dropped his gaze to the screen in front of him and opened his email. Scrolling through his new messages, he found one from the Ranger he'd given the job of collecting all the statements from the various card companies.

Clicking on the attachment, he downloaded it to his files and opened it along with the other electronic statements he had from the other victims' cards. He did a search for Tim's Gym.

"Shit. I'm not sure it's anything more than a coincidence," he muttered as he scrolled through the different papers.

"Why?" Tanner didn't move from where he stood at the table.

"Because only two of them charged something at Tim's Gym. The other three have charges to gyms, but they're different ones. Not even really in the same areas of town." He pushed the computer away from him and stood, pacing the floor. "I don't believe he's picking them randomly. If he was, he wouldn't be stalking them for days before he grabs them."

Tanner shook his head. "He's not doing any of this randomly. He's organized, not only in his actions, but in his thoughts as well. Each action is thought out beforehand. He knows where he's taking them once he grabs them. He knows where he's going to dump them once he's killed them. Each woman is killed by the same number of strokes."

"What? Why didn't you say that during our meeting with MacLaughlin and Billingsley?" Macario propped his fists on his hips and glared at Tanner. "It might have been important."

"It is important, but not to discovering his identity. It helps me form a profile of his psyche. That's all. Trust me, if I thought it would help give you an idea of who he is, I'd have told you as soon as I figured it out." Tanner turned and met his gaze. "I'm surprised one of you didn't catch on to that. It's in the ME's reports."

"I haven't had a chance to go through all of them yet. Sorensterm was the lead on those." Macario shoved his hand through his hair. "Not a good enough excuse, is it?"

"Not really." Tanner nodded toward the files. "You should pull them out and read through them. Marissa's arrived today. The ME put a rush on it because any new information we can get will help."

Macario held his hand over Marissa's file and hesitated. "Shit, I don't want to know all the fucked-up stuff he did to her."

Tanner gripped Macario's shoulder tight. "I know, but I can tell you, he didn't do anything different to her than he did to the others. I will say Marissa must have been more difficult than the others. She sustained more cuts than the other women. While the wounds were within the thirty to forty amount, it was higher than the others."

"Why?" Not sure what emotion prompted him, Macario reached up and entwined his fingers with Tanner's.

"Why what? Why was her count higher than the others? Or why does he only cut them between thirty and forty times?" Tanner sat next to him and pressed close, their hands dropping to lie on his thigh.

"Both, I guess." Macario didn't want to hear how she'd died. How scared she'd been and how much pain she'd been in. He didn't want to think about how he hadn't been able to save her. It didn't matter that he hadn't even known she was in danger until it was too late. He still felt like he should have done something to keep her alive.

"It wasn't your fault," Tanner murmured as he laid his head on Macario's shoulder.

Macario shrugged his other shoulder. "It feels like it is. I've been working this case for four months, I should have something on him, and we can warn women about him."

"That's not how things work, Macario, and you know it. If you haven't caught him within the first forty-eight hours of the killing, then it's going to get harder and harder to find him."

"For your usual murder case," he pointed out.

Tanner stroked his thumb over Macario's knuckles. "But in a serial murder case, you have to treat each victim as a separate case while you're gathering evidence. Sure, there are a ton of clues to connect it to the other murders, but who's to say that with the latest one, he didn't get sloppy. Maybe someone saw him around Marissa right before she disappeared or someone saw his vehicle. Once you have him on one case, you connect him to the others."

Macario dropped his head and stared at the carpet under his feet. "In my mind, I know all this and I know it's not my fault that Marissa died, but my heart's a different story. She's the only person I ever chose to care about."

"You didn't even love your ex-wife? Was it bad from the beginning?" Tanner's low question held hesitation, like he wasn't sure Macario would answer.

He closed his eyes and exhaled loudly. "No. I picked her because she was good-looking and Mexican. It made José happy and that's all I cared about. We got along all right in bed."

Tanner started to say something, but Macario interrupted him.

"I'm gay, but that doesn't mean I can't function with women. It just means they don't do as much for me as men do."

"Wouldn't that make you bisexual then?" Tanner seemed puzzled about Macario's ability to fuck women.

"No. I slept with them because I thought that's what I was supposed to do. Hell, there were times when it didn't matter what sex my partner was, as long as they were willing and warm, I fucked them." He grimaced. "Not particularly proud of that, but it's what I did."

"But you never formed an attachment to any of them? No relationships or friendships for that matter?"

He shook his head. "No. I don't have a lot of friends. Marissa was the only person I really cared about and she's gone now. See why I don't get emotionally involved with people. Some way or another, they always leave, even if they don't mean to do it."

Tanner remained quiet. Had he offended the man or was Tanner trying to figure out a way to back out of what was happening between them? Macario admitted to himself he liked Tanner way more than he should, and wasn't that fucked up. They'd only met two days ago, and already they were lovers, yet even without the intense attraction he felt for the agent, Macario knew they'd have been friends.

"I don't know anything about your background, except what you told me." Tanner held up his hand to stop Macario. "And I don't need to know any of it unless you want to enlighten me. But from what you've said, I guess I understand how you feel about Marissa and about caring for people. No one I loved ever walked away from me. I didn't know my father, so his leaving didn't affect me much, unless you count clinging tighter to my mother."

Silence reigned in the room for a few minutes as Macario thought about his mother. He didn't know much about her, just that the authorities had taken him away from her when he was five because she was an addict. He never wanted to know anything more about her. He rubbed his chin with his free hand and sighed.

"We need to get some work done. I need something to give to Billingsley tomorrow."

Tanner laughed softly and pushed to his feet. "Tell him you think he's picking them up at gyms, or at least that's where he finds them."

Macario shot Tanner a surprised glance. "Gyms? What makes you say that? Only two of them went to Tim's Gym."

"I didn't say he found them at the same gym, just that he finds them at gyms. I think if you go through all the bills for each girl, you'll discover they all had memberships. It might not seem like a big deal since they didn't all go to the same one, but trust me, I've got a hunch that's where he starts."

With that pronouncement, Tanner strolled back to the dining room table and began to stare at the photos again. Macario studied Tanner's straight back for a moment before turning to his computer and doing what Tanner had suggested.

He searched through credit card statements and other bills gathered in the victims' names. Still only two had gym memberships listed. Macario frowned, but kept digging. Tanner knew what he was doing, and even though they'd only just met, Macario trusted Tanner's instincts already.

An hour later, he found what he was looking for and shouted.

"Hot damn!" He entered the information on the main case file page before highlighting it on each victim's file. "You were right, Tanner. They all went to the gym."

Tanner didn't reply and Macario twisted around to see what the man was doing. Tanner stood in almost the exact same position as an hour before, still staring at the photos. After standing, he walked over to where Tanner stood and got a glimpse of what he studied.

The enlarged copies of the wound carved into each

woman's breast were laid out on the table with each victim's headshot. The carvings stood out red against the rather pale flesh of each victim and Macario winced at the amount of pain they must have felt while the killer did that.

"They were dead when he did it." Tanner didn't look away from the gallery of photos.

"How did you know what I was thinking?" He leaned closer to Tanner, absorbing the man's warmth and musky scent.

"I thought the same thing when I first saw it on the fifth victim's chest, but as I traced the lines, I realized there wasn't any blood anywhere around the wound. This is his true ritual. This is the one thing that he must complete the same way each time." Tanner trailed his finger around the outside edge of each swirl. "This is what's going to help us catch him. We study this mark and we'll begin to understand why he does what he does."

Macario didn't think the carving would be able to help them that much, but Tanner was the profiler and if he believed it would help find the bastard, Macario would let him draw that fucking design over and over.

Checking his watch, he saw it was closing in on eleven. Somehow they had spent several hours digging through the files and they had one thing to show for it. Which was better than what they'd had earlier. They'd found the connection between the victims and while they still didn't know why he picked them, they at least knew where he found them.

"Time to call it a night," he said as he slid his arm around Tanner's waist and tugged the man close to him.

Tanner turned into his embrace while slipping his arms over Macario's shoulders. "Oh really? You really want to go home and sleep? Or do you want to find a way to make you so tired, you won't dream tonight?"

"Mmm...I have to say I'm not looking forward to driving home to an empty bed. Maybe I should take you up on your offer to tire me out enough to sleep." He nuzzled Tanner's jaw, leaving wet kisses along his chin to the soft skin behind

Tanner's ear. He placed a sucking bite there, and Tanner shuddered.

"Trust me. I'll make it very good for you."

Chapter Six

Tanner threaded his fingers through the hair at the nape of Macario's neck and drew the man's mouth to his. Yeah, he'd do his best to wear Macario out. He wanted the detective to sleep well that night. Violent dreams and nightmares would haunt Tanner's nights until the case was over—or longer—until they slowly faded to join the other cases he'd worked.

He mentally blocked all those thoughts and sank into the kiss. He let Macario take control, not fighting when Macario led him from the living room to the bedroom. *Ah, a man after my own heart.*

They stripped in comfortable silence, no discussion needed on where this was going. Tanner pulled the lube and rubbers from the nightstand and tossed them on the mattress before he climbed on the bed. Lying on his back, he spread his legs.

"Is this how you want me?" He grinned and stroked his cock while Macario caressed every inch of his body with his heated gaze.

"At some point tonight, but I think I want your mouth around my dick at the moment." Macario leered.

"Okay." Tanner scrambled through the sheets for the rubbers. He tore one from the trio and tossed it at Macario. "Put that on and get up here."

A low growl filled the air as Macario did just that. Settling back, Tanner let Macario straddle his chest, placing his knees in Tanner's armpits and bracing one hand on the headboard in front of him. Tanner grabbed Macario's ass and urged him to lean forward.

Macario positioned the flared head of his erection at Tanner's mouth and slowly sank in. Tanner relaxed his throat and swallowed as much of Macario's length as he could the first time. Thank God, he'd managed to eliminate most of his gag reflex throughout the years of giving blow jobs. Macario didn't stop until his balls hit Tanner's chin.

He raised his gaze and met Macario's dark eyes. Something gleamed in them, but Macario blinked and it disappeared. He tapped the firm ass muscles in his hands, giving Macario the signal to move. Macario wrapped both hands around the top of Tanner's headboard and started sliding back.

Tanner applied suction, making sure to tease the heated flesh in his mouth with his tongue when he could. He didn't like the latex taste, but dealt with it. No point in getting careless, even if he did trust Macario.

While Macario plunged in and out of his mouth, Tanner played his fingers over the warm skin of Macario's ass, dipping between the cheeks to rub over the man's puckered opening. Macario shivered and pushed back, giving Tanner the impression he wanted more. Not wanting to breach Macario dry, Tanner removed one of his hands from Macario's body to search for the lube.

Macario protested, but when he figured out what Tanner was doing, he snatched the slick and popped the top. He gestured for Tanner to hold out his hand, which Tanner did. A generous amount of lube squirted into his palm and he began to coat his fingers with it. With that taken care of, Macario began fucking Tanner's mouth again. Tanner wished he could taste the salty skin covered by the condom. Maybe some day, if their relationship lasted beyond this case and beyond all of Tanner's secrets.

He pressed his finger against Macario's hole, and his lover pushed back. They both moaned as Tanner invaded the tight ring of muscle, sinking in up to his middle knuckle. There had to be some burning because Macario was tight, like the man didn't give up his ass very often.

Yet Macario didn't stop, even if there was some discomfort. He rocked between Tanner's mouth and finger.

"More," Macario demanded and Tanner figured he meant more fingers, so he added another.

Within a few minutes, Tanner had three fingers inside Macario's ass, stretching the puckered opening because he planned on riding the man hard. He angled his fingers just right and nailed Macario's gland.

"Fuck!"

Macario jerked and Tanner grinned around Macario's cock as the man shot a glance down at him.

"Stop." Macario shifted, sliding out of Tanner's mouth and away from his fingers.

"But—" Tanner grabbed for him.

Macario shook his head. "We're getting a rubber on you, man, and you'll fuck me. I want to come on your cock."

No way was he going to argue about that. He tore open a foil package and rolled the condom on without delay. How fast could he get inside Macario? Tanner pushed the man over onto his back and wedged his hips between Macario's thighs. His lover brought his legs up to his chest and spread them, giving him more access.

"Are you sure?" He met Macario's intense gaze.

"Just fuck me, Tanner. Don't overthink this shit."

He nodded and slammed home, burying himself balls deep in Macario's ass. Macario threw his head back and bit his bottom lip. Tanner froze, not wanting to move until Macario told him it was okay. After a few seconds, Macario's inner muscles contracted around Tanner's shaft and Tanner gasped as Macario gripped his ass with rough hands to jerk Tanner toward him.

"I need you to move, man. Move fast, hard, and soon." Macario snarled at him.

Tanner bit back a laugh and did just as Macario had demanded. He reamed Macario good and hard, thrusting in as deep as he could get before pulling back. They moved together to the best music in the world—grunts, groans and skin hitting skin. The air grew hot around them, coating them with sweat and filling the room with the scent of sex.

He became lost in the rhythm of their lovemaking. The hard muscles flexing under his hands as he held Macario's hips. The way Macario's breath caught in his chest every time Tanner filled him. How Macario closed his eyes right before he came.

Tanner's eyes rolled back in his head as Macario clamped down on his cock and massaged the entire length, demanding Tanner's climax. His balls drew tight to his body as all the pleasure rocketed through him and he flooded the condom.

They trembled together as the aftershocks raced through them. Tanner collapsed onto Macario with a muffled apology. Macario patted his butt lightly.

"I'll clean us both off when my brain sends signals to my muscles again," he muttered, burying his nose into the crook of Macario's neck.

"No big deal. Maybe we both can stumble into the bathroom and take a shower. It'll be quicker."

Macario's suggestion sounded good to Tanner, so he made a concentrated effort to roll over. Macario groaned and winced a little as Tanner's softened cock slid from him.

"Are you okay? I didn't hurt you, did I?" Tanner rested his hand on Macario's chest.

"No. I'm fine, but I'll definitely be feeling what we did tomorrow." Macario yawned. "Let's get the shower done quickly. I'm about out on my feet, kind of."

Tanner managed to get up without falling to the floor. He held out his hand and helped Macario up. They wobbled their way to the bathroom where they disposed of the condoms and took a quick hot shower. After drying off, they wandered back to bed and slipped under the covers.

Macario fell asleep almost as soon as his head hit the pillow. Tanner snuggled close to his lover, arm over the man's waist, but he didn't sleep right away. He stared at the wall, his mind racing. What would happen if Macario ever found out the truth about Tanner's family? Would the cop in Macario take over and decide it was a security risk to date Tanner? Or would Macario trust Tanner enough to realize Tanner would never sabotage a case because of family loyalty?

Sighing, he closed his eyes and decided to worry about it later. His concerns might be unfounded because Macario had never said anything about them dating after the case was over. Maybe their fucking was just a result of the emotional loss Macario had suffered, and when the killer was captured, Macario would turn away from him. Tanner cleared his mind and tried to relax. Soon his exhaustion caught up with him and he drifted into slumber.

* * * *

The precise swirls whirled around Tanner's head, drawing closer and closer to him with each twist. He tried to duck, but he couldn't move and the sting of a blade slicing into his chest shocked him. Warm liquid trickled down over his pectoral muscles and dripped to the floor. He hung from something, but when he opened his eyes, it was dark.

It's a dream, *his mind warned him, but the pain made it feel real. The sharp knife carved the design into his skin and Tanner bit his lip to keep from yelling.* It's a dream, *he kept telling himself, wanting to struggle and get away, but knowing he wouldn't be able to.*

Suddenly the tip of the knife bit deeper in the middle of the design as the killer carved something there. Just as Tanner believed. There was something hidden inside the swirls and circles, even his subconscious, which was directing this dream, had it figured out. He winced and jerked.

His hands broke free and Tanner awoke as his body plummeted from the wall it hung on. He hit the floor beside the bed with a thud. Standing, he grimaced and rubbed his ass. Macario didn't react, saving Tanner from acute embarrassment. He dug out a pair of sweats and slipped them on before leaving the bedroom.

After turning on the light over the dining table, he stood for a second, staring at the carvings. He wished there was a way to get pictures of it from every angle. Maybe he just wasn't looking at it the right way. Tanner put a teakettle on in the kitchen since he knew he wouldn't be going back to sleep.

It was four in the morning and his mind had decided he needed to be working on the case. Something else bothered him about the killings. Macario had been right. There weren't any other unsolved crimes like this one in the database, but there were several killings scattered across the Southwest committed by the same person—or so the authorities believed.

They had definitely been done by a person with an affinity to knives, but the local LEOs had attributed them to drug killings. A drug mule or dealer getting full of himself, or skimming off the profits, and the cartel sent in an enforcer to take care of the problem.

Yet none of the crime scene or ME's reports said anything about a design carved into the victim's body and that a single slice across the throat killed all of the victims. He sat down at his laptop and brought up his email. Contacting the investigating officers from the different cases might get him more information, or even photos from the scenes. While nothing about the female victims suggested they had anything to do with drugs or the lifestyle, Tanner wasn't willing to dismiss any possibility. Who was to say the perp in the drug cases hadn't graduated to being a serial killer?

Drug enforcers were serial killers in their own way. Most of them didn't have rituals in their violence, but they killed without guilt or fear. Drug killings were often violent and bloody to send a message to anyone thinking about double-crossing the cartels.

He sent out several requests, but he knew it could take a few days to hear back. Tanner wandered into the kitchen and made a mug of tea before returning to the photos. Why kill them at one place before moving them to another? Why take the risk of being seen at any point during the whole process?

There wasn't any evidence in the warehouses where the bodies had been found that he killed them there. No other rooms in the buildings were found to have been used by anyone other than squatters. Where did he kill them? Was where he killed them part of his ritual or was where he dumped them? Did it even matter? What if the most important part of the whole killing was the carving on their chest, and everything else was just stupid shit to throw the investigators off the scent?

Tanner gathered all the crime scene photos, not including the ones of the bodies, and went to curl up on the couch. He'd looked at the actual body photos enough for now. It was time to look at the rest of the room. Maybe something would stand out and he'd be able to add more to his profile.

When he heard movement from his bedroom an hour later, he glanced up to see Macario leaning in the doorway of the living room. One shoulder braced against the wall, Macario wore his pants, and nothing else. Tanner licked his lips at the picture of sheer sensuality his lover made, bare-chested and rumpled from sleep.

"How long have you been up?" Macario shuffled over to the couch then dropped down on it, picking Tanner's feet up and laying them in his lap.

Tanner rested his cheek on the back of the couch and studied Macario's face. "About an hour or so. Had a nightmare and knew I wouldn't be getting back to sleep anytime soon. So I figured I'd come out here and try to get some more work done."

He didn't worry about looking weak in front of Macario. The Ranger probably had his own nightmares to deal with from past cases.

"Why didn't you wake me? I would have been happy to take your mind off your dreams." Macario ran his hand up Tanner's calf to his knee and back, massaging as he went.

Tanner closed his eyes as he savored the warmth of Macario's fingers on his body. "Didn't see the point of both of us losing sleep, even though having sex with you would have been great. I know you've been running on less sleep than me, and didn't want to disturb you. Also, I was going to get you up soon anyway."

"Yeah. I've got to head home and change before meeting Billingsley and briefing him on what we figured out." Macario didn't seem in too big a hurry to leave.

"He should be happy you have new leads to work on. Oh, by the way, I'll be coming to look through all the physical evidence you took from the scenes at some point today. I want to make sure I'm not overlooking anything that might help add to his profile."

Macario nodded. "Give me a call before you come and I'll make sure the boxes are available to you. I think the ME's going to release Marissa's body today. I told the Levistens I'd call them when they could have the funeral home come get her."

Tanner took Macario's hand in his and squeezed. "I know it's going to be difficult. You know my number and you can call me any time to talk, or just to bitch about how bad the Texans are playing."

Macario's rough chuckle rippled over Tanner's body. "I know it and I'll probably be calling you to meet me at a bar, so I can get rip-roaring drunk tonight."

"Ah, but I know better. You won't get drunk until this case is over and the bastard's been caught. When that happens, we'll go out and I'll buy the first round." He entwined their fingers and let their hands settle on his shin.

"I like the fact you said when, and not if." Macario closed his eyes and leaned his head back.

"Do you really think there's even a remote possibility you won't find who did this?" Tanner shook his head. "Macario, you won't rest until the man who killed Marissa is behind bars. I might not have known you for very long, but I think I understand how tenacious you are when it comes to cases.

You wouldn't be where you're at in the Rangers if you didn't solve a lot of your cases."

"And you wouldn't be where you're at if you weren't good at your job," Macario remarked, opening his eyes to meet Tanner's gaze. "Between the two of us, we'll bring the fucker down. He might kill another woman, but it'll be his last. I'm not letting him hurt another person after that."

Tanner brought Macario's hand up to his mouth and pressed a kiss on the man's knuckles. "I wish there was a way to save this last one, but unless we get a miracle, I don't see it."

"I know, yet with each murder, he risks screwing up. No one's perfect a hundred percent of the time, and we'll catch him because of that."

"Why did you become a cop in the first place?" Tanner shrugged when Macario looked at him. "I don't know why, but it's not the first career choice I'd think of for you."

Macario's smile looked more like a smirk. "What do you think I should be doing?"

"Don't know for sure, but my instincts tell me if José hadn't gotten to you, you'd be on the other side of the law. Probably not a mule though. You'd be in the middle of whatever criminal activity you chose."

He burst out laughing as Macario shoved him onto his back and loomed over him. He spread his legs, letting Macario's hips nestle between them. Reaching up, he smoothed the hair falling over Macario's forehead.

"You're right, even after José adopted me, I was still rather wild. Then I met a cop who used to come into José's store. We'd talk and he convinced me that police work was interesting and at times, could be exciting."

"What did you do when you found out he exaggerated about how fast-paced and exciting a cop's life could be?" Tanner trailed his fingers down over Macario's nose and outlined his lips.

Macario nipped at Tanner's finger. "By the time I figured it out, it was too late. I'd already graduated from the academy, plus he knew what made me tick deep inside and what would make me a good detective."

"What was that?" Tanner murmured, losing a little interest in their conversation as Macario ground his erection against Tanner's.

"I like puzzles, and solving them. I like getting all the pieces, putting them together, and getting the final picture. That's what makes me a good investigator. I can't stand not knowing things. I'm always digging into things, even stuff that doesn't concern me."

Tanner stiffened slightly. What if Macario decided he wanted to know more about Tanner? What if he dug deep into Tanner's past? He'd never really worried about someone finding out about his family history. Not even when he'd joined the Bureau. His mother had told him they were safe, and he'd accepted her word for it.

Macario leaned down and nuzzled Tanner's jaw, causing him to lift his head to allow Macario kiss a line along his throat. He whimpered softly as Macario scraped his teeth over Tanner's jugular. He kept one hand on Macario's shoulder and gripped the back of the couch with the other one. Tanner arched up as Macario licked one of his nipples.

"Shit." He shuddered when his lover pinched the hard nub with his teeth. "I'm not sure if this is the best time. You need to get home and changed before you go into work."

His weak protest drew a rumbling sound from Macario. Tanner managed to open his eyes and met Macario's. One more teasing nibble then Macario eased away. Tanner flopped back, covering his face with his arm.

"Why have I suddenly become diligent about work? I should have just kept my mouth shut," he complained.

"Come on. You're right, and we'll pick up where I left off later." Macario held out his hand to help Tanner off the couch.

"Do you want a cup of coffee to go?" Tanner paused. "I can brew a cup for you."

"I thought you didn't drink coffee," Macario said over his

shoulder as he headed to the bedroom.

"I don't anymore, but I still keep some on hand in case I have guests who do." Tanner pursed his lips. "It's a new can of coffee. I threw out the last one since I don't tend to have a lot of guests over."

"Sure. If you don't mind." Macario's voice disappeared when he entered the bedroom.

"No problem." He got everything ready and brewing before making his way back to the bedroom.

Macario was in the bathroom when Tanner got there. After pulling out a dress shirt and tie, Tanner stood at his dresser and listened to the water running in the sink. It had been a long time since he'd had any guy spend the night. Usually he'd either go over to their place or he'd kick them out right after the sex was done. Yet the thought had never occurred to him last night or the night before to toss Macario out when they'd finished. What made the man so different from the others?

"Oh, you got a text or something. Your phone beeping woke me up. Sorry about not telling you sooner." Macario came out of the bathroom, buttoning his shirt.

"Thanks." Tanner fought the urge to rush over and check his phone. It wasn't his work one, since that had been out in the living room with him. He grabbed some briefs from the dresser and tossed them on the bed. "You heading out?"

"Yeah."

Macario encircled Tanner's waist, drawing him close. Their lips came together in a gentle kiss, more like 'good morning' and 'have a good day' than 'let's fuck right now'. Tanner played with the damp hairs at the base of Macario's skull. Their tongues stroked along each other and Tanner shivered as his cock hardened. One more quick kiss then Macario stepped away.

"If we don't stop now, we'll be in bed until noon and we'll both get our asses chewed."

As much as he hated to agree, he did. "You're right. Get going. I'll call you when I'm ready to come over and look at the physical evidence."

"See you later then." Macario slapped him on the ass as he walked by.

"Jackass," Tanner grumbled, rubbing the offended cheek.

He waited until the front door had shut behind Macario before picking up his personal phone from the nightstand. Sitting on the edge of the bed, he scrolled through for missed messages. His hand shook slightly, hoping it wasn't bad news.

Back in Houston. Small emergency.

Shit! He typed quickly. *Everyone ok?*

Tanner wanted to pace, but kept his body still. No reason to worry. There probably wasn't anything wrong, and really, even if there was, he couldn't do anything about it. Not without losing his job and probably coming under investigation himself.

Fine. Business related.

He breathed a sigh of relief. *Thx for letting me know. B careful.*

Always.

After shutting his phone, he tossed it on the mattress next to him. He braced his elbows on his knees and studied the carpet. He needed to take the time soon to decide if he wanted to keep his life the way it was. It got harder and harder to keep everything separate, and unless he wanted to cut out a very important part of his life, he knew what he had to do.

Tanner stood and shoved his hands through his hair, vowing to seriously think about his future after the case was solved. His phone beeped again. He flipped it open and checked the text.

Lilies.

A smile crossed his face as he typed. *Got it.*

He dropped the phone onto the sheets before stripping as he strolled into the bathroom. He needed to get dressed and go to work. He had to type up his profile and take it over to Macario, plus he had some other cases to go over with Sam. It was going to be a busy day, but he'd take lunch and go visit his mother's grave. He tried to get there once a week, just to say hi. It might seem a little creepy, but he liked to go to the cemetery. An odd sense of peace filled the air and he always came back refreshed to face the terrible crimes he investigated.

He snorted and climbed under the hot water. God, he was weird. Probably why he'd ended up in the Behavioral Science Unit of the FBI instead of a regular agent. At certain times, Tanner thought he was going out of his mind with how easily he connected with the serial killers and mass murderers he interviewed. Each time it got easier to understand how they killed and why.

Tanner ducked his head and let the water wash away his thoughts. He needed to focus on the Knife case, and not worry about his own mind. He had all the time in the world afterward to clean the images out of his brain.

* * * *

Around one o'clock, he drove through the gates at Sacred Heart Cemetery and wound his way to the section where his mother was buried. After climbing out, he strolled over to her headstone.

He smiled as he reached out to touch the bouquet of lilies resting against it. "He loves you so much, Mama, and while having him around complicates my life, I'm happy that he's here. He thinks I need to be watched over, protected like a little boy, but I don't."

Sitting cross-legged on the ground, he pressed his hand to the headstone. "I met someone, and I think you would've liked him. He's a lonely soul, growing up in foster system made him that way, but I do think he wants to reach out. He wants to love someone. He just hasn't found the right one."

A gentle breeze brushed over his cheek and he laughed. "I'm not saying I'm the right one for him, Mama, but you never know what might happen."

After unwrapping his sandwich, Tanner ate while allowing the peace of the cemetery to fill his soul. He always felt safe and clean after visiting his mother's grave. While she wasn't on earth with him anymore, she was still only one of three people who knew his secrets, so he could be himself when he was there.

Once lunch was done, he crumbled up all his trash and pressed his hand to her headstone one last time, then made his way back to the car. He still had work to do on the case, but the quiet had given him strength to continue doing his job.

Chapter Seven

Macario crumbled the list of gyms in his hand as he saw the Levistens walk into the bullpen at Company 'A's headquarter. *Shit!* He'd forgotten to call them earlier about being able to get Marissa's body. He threw the papers on his desk and went to intercept them.

"Mr. and Mrs. Levisten, I'm sorry I didn't call you like I said I would. I got the release notice from the ME last night and I've been busy with a slight break in the case this morning."

He held out his hand and Marissa's father shook it.

"We understand, Macario. We'd prefer you focus on who killed our daughter. You said you had a break in the case?" Mr. Levisten looked at him eagerly.

"I can't go into details, but it moves us closer to finding the person who did this to Marissa. I'll call down to the morgue and have someone come up to help you make arrangements to get Marissa's body to the funeral home." He gestured toward his desk. "If you'd like to sit down while you wait."

After getting them coffee, he called down to the coroner's office and arranged for someone to come and collect the Levistens. He hung up and sat down next to Mrs. Levisten. Her wan smile tugged at his heart.

"I'm terribly sorry about all of this, Mrs. Levisten."

She patted his hand. "It's not your fault, Macario. You had no way of knowing that monster was stalking our daughter. Do you know when we'll be able to get back into her apartment? I need to get some clothes for her to be buried in."

He winced internally at the thought. "Let me check."

After shifting through his papers, he read one note and nodded. "You can go in. We've picked up what evidence we think we might need from there."

"Thank you."

"Ranger Guzman."

Macario stood when Tanner spoke from behind him. Turning, he met his lover's gaze and something in his face must have told Tanner the people sitting with him were important.

"Agent Wallace." They shook hands, and Macario turned back to the older couple. "This is Mr. and Mrs. Levisten, Marissa's parents."

"I'm sorry for your loss." Tanner shook hands with both of them. Somehow he managed to make those trite words sincere.

"Are you working with Macario on the case?" Mr. Levisten asked.

Macario spotted the coroner's assistant and waved her over.

"Yes, I am. There's an entire task force trying to catch the man who did this. We're getting closer every day. I'm going to tell Major Billingsley I'm here. I wish we could have met under better circumstances." Tanner dipped his head toward them before heading in the direction of Billingsley's office.

"Here's Ms. Powell from the ME's office. She'll help you with all the paperwork and everything you need." Macario handed Marissa's parents off to the lady. "Please let me know when her funeral is."

"We will. Thank you again, Macario."

He watched the Levistens follow Ms. Powell until they disappeared into the elevator. After they left, he scooped up the list of gyms and stalked to the major's office. Knocking on the door, he waited to hear Billingsley call for him to come in. He walked in and spotted Tanner leaning a hip on Billingsley's desk while gesturing with his hands.

He paused as both men turned to look at him. Billingsley folded his arms over his chest and raised an eyebrow.

"Is there something you neglected to tell me, Guzman?"

Shooting a quick glance at Tanner, he got no hint from the man's blank expression. "I'm not sure what you mean, Cap."

"I was informed a little while ago that you knew the last victim, Marissa Levisten."

Tanner shook his head when Macario looked at him again. Billingsley set his narrow-eyed gaze on Tanner.

"Did you know this, Agent Wallace?"

"Yes, sir." Tanner slid off the desk and moved to stand next to Macario. "I thought Guzman could remain objective enough to do the work needed to catch the perp."

"Yes, sir. I did know Marissa." Macario stood, hands clasped behind his back. "When I was fifteen, I lived with the Levistens for six months. They were foster parents in the system out in California. Unfortunately for me, Mr. Levisten got a new job out of state, and I couldn't move with them. I got kicked back into the system."

Billingsley still didn't look happy. "Why didn't you say anything when her body was discovered? Why didn't you help us identify her? You wasted valuable police time that could have been used for research."

He took a deep breath and swallowed the urge to make excuses. "I'm sorry, sir. I should have come straight to you as soon as I realized it was Marissa. I was afraid you'd remove me from the case and I really want to catch this guy."

"It's personal now?" Billingsley asked.

Macario grimaced. "No, sir. It was personal before Marissa was killed. Any case I get becomes personal to me. I work twenty-four-seven if I have to, on any case."

His statement must have been what Billingsley wanted to hear because the major relaxed slightly. His own tension eased and he pulled the list from behind his back.

"I brought the list of gyms our victims used. Only two

went to the same one, but we think that's how he's finding them." He nodded toward Tanner.

"Okay. Take Sorensterm and go ask questions at those gyms. See if anyone remembers seeing anything unusual around the time each victim disappeared. Oh, and Agent Wallace said you were going to get him access to the physical evidence from the case."

"Yes, sir. Tanner thinks the evidence might give him some more stuff to add to the profile he's writing."

"I just gave the major my preliminary report. There's a copy in there for you as well." Tanner pointed to the file sitting on Billingsley's desk. "It's everything I found from looking at the photos and reading the crime scene descriptions. As we go along, I'll be adding more to it until it's fleshed out as much as it can be."

"Good. Now get out of here and find the killer for me." Billingsley waved them out of the office. "Oh, and Mac, don't ever keep something like this away from me again, or I'll have your badge."

"Yes, sir."

They shut the door behind them, and Macario grabbed Tanner's arm, dragging him down the hallway to an empty room. He pulled Tanner in with him. After making sure the door was closed, he whirled back around.

"What the hell was that?"

Tanner frowned and sat on the edge of the table, arms folded. "I don't know."

"You didn't say a word to anyone about me knowing Marissa?"

"I probably should be insulted you'd think I'd run to your major behind your back, but I guess since you don't know me that well, I'll give you the benefit of the doubt." Tanner rolled his eyes. "Of course I didn't say anything. Why would I when it would get me in trouble as well?"

"Sorry. I'm just trying to figure out how he would have found out so soon." Macario paced the room.

"You were going to tell him about the connection between

you and Marissa, weren't you?" Tanner shot the question at him.

He nodded. "Yeah. I really would have told him eventually. I wonder how he found out."

"More than likely, the Levistens said something about knowing you. You know, you can't really hide things in your past, especially from law enforcement." Tanner paused and something flickered in his eyes before he continued, "At least he didn't pull you from the case."

"Yeah, even though I deserve it for not saying anything." Macario scrubbed his hand over his face. "Okay. I need to take you to the evidence room before I grab Sorensterm and head out to interview people."

Tanner snagged Macario's arm as he walked past him. Swinging toward Tanner, Macario opened his mouth to say something, but Tanner covered his mouth with his own. Macario stiffened, aware that on the other side of the door were his fellow Rangers. Before he could push Tanner away, Tanner let him go.

"Let's go. You want to meet at my place for dinner tonight? We'll regroup and see what we've got." Tanner glanced back at him as he walked toward the door. "And quit freaking out. I wouldn't have done that if we weren't alone. I'm not interested in 'outing' you, if none of them know you're gay."

"It's not really that," Macario mumbled. "I just don't like public displays of affection. Not used to them, either."

"You should get used to them, especially if we go out to the clubs." Tanner winked at him before opening the door and walking out.

Macario winced slightly, but followed the man. He lifted his gaze from Tanner's jean-covered ass when they joined the other Rangers out in the main room. Sorensterm stood next to Macario's desk.

"Billingsley said you had a lead to work on."

"Yeah. We're going to check out some gyms. Seems like all our victims worked out, and it might be where our guy spots them." Macario picked up a copy of the list and handed it to Sorensterm. "I thought we could go and question the people there. See if they noticed anything weird, or if they even remember the women."

"Good idea." Sorensterm looked at Tanner. "What's the Fed doing here?"

Tanner rolled his eyes, but kept his mouth shut. Macario snorted silently.

"He's going through all the physical evidence from the crime scenes. Never know what he might find."

"Do you really think you're going to find something we haven't?" Sorensterm rested his fists on his hips and stared Tanner down.

Macario bit his lip. Tanner could take care of himself and it wouldn't look good if Macario stood up for him. He opened the top drawer of his desk and pulled out his gun and holster.

"I might find something you didn't think was important. As a cop, you're looking for clues to identify the killer. As a profiler, I'm looking for anything that will help me to get inside his head. Even the most insignificant item could help me give you a better profile to work from." Tanner shrugged. "I'm not saying you aren't doing your job, Sorensterm. I'm simply saying I'm looking for different things than you are."

"I'm willing to use any option at our disposal to catch this bastard. If he wants to waste his time looking through evidence we already looked through, then good for him." Macario clipped his gun to his belt and grabbed his hat from the hook on the wall. "Let's get going. It's going to be a long day."

"Good luck. I'll get someone to take me to the evidence locker. I'll talk to you later, Guzman." Tanner nodded to both of them as they walked away.

Macario watched the agent for a few seconds before giving himself a mental shake and gestured to Sorensterm. "You can drive."

"Where are we going?"

"We're going to Tim's Gym to start with." He gave Sorensterm the address. "We think he's picking them out at the gyms. We still don't know why he chooses the ones he does, but it's a place to start."

Sorensterm grunted, but didn't say anything else about the case. "I got a hold of Snap and we're setting up a game on Friday. Figure we all are going to need a break. Snap's having a problem with the Delarosa cartel case."

"Will they ever catch the man? Not that they have any proof he's done anything wrong." Macario snorted. "That's what all his lieutenants and minions are for."

"Must be the first thing they teach you at drug kingpin school, huh? Always make sure you have people below you on the ladder to ensure you don't ever go to jail." Sorensterm signed out one of the cars and they climbed in.

"It has to be frustrating because Delarosa has a better communication network than Snap does. When they get there to arrest him, he's already been gone for forty minutes." Macario grimaced. "I wish we had such good communications."

"Probably help get things done quicker around here." Sorensterm chuckled as he pulled out into traffic.

"True." Macario looked through the pictures of the victims. "Do you think this perp's mistake is going to be he picked two girls from the same gym?"

"Stranger things have caught serial killers." Sorensterm shot a look over at Macario. "Do you really think the Bureau guy is going to give us better information than our own profiler?"

Macario shrugged. "He's already helped point out that the guy might be finding his victims at gyms, not that we wouldn't have come to that conclusion ourselves. But Wallace isn't interested in getting any glory for himself. He's quite happy working in the background."

Sorensterm coughed slightly, but didn't say anything else.

"Listen, our profiler's good. Hell, he got trained at

Quantico, but he doesn't have as much experience as Wallace does. Like I said, I'll take all the help I can get to find this guy." Macario shuffled through the files. "Let's go over the case again."

"Okay." Sorensterm didn't sound happy, though Macario doubted he'd keep complaining about Tanner working with them. Sorensterm might not like the Bureau, but the man was a good cop and understood doing whatever it took to solve the case.

* * * *

Everything was set. He'd cleaned the room and set up everything for his newest guest. It was time to get her and bring her to his place. It would be easy since she'd never once noticed him following her. Stupid bitch. Didn't she understand there were dangerous people out there just waiting to take advantage of her unobservant nature?

He resisted the urge to rub his hands together in glee. The need to feel the shock of his blade cutting through flesh and the warmth of blood coating his hands built until he could barely contain the pressure. The voice in his mind telling him to do it had grown louder until there wasn't anything else left except the want for someone dying by his own hand.

Damn his former boss for firing him. If the fucker hadn't given him his walking papers, he'd have had another outlet for this need. Oh, he'd thought about going after the man, but there wasn't any way he'd be able to get close enough to kill the way he needed.

A knife let him get up close and personal with his victims. He loved seeing the fear in their eyes when they realized he wasn't going to just rape them and let them go. The shock as he sliced them for the first time, and the dull resignation in their face when they understood they were going to die, hanging like a piece of meat in the kill room.

Oh, but his last victim had been the best so far. She'd

fought for so long and so hard, he'd actually thought he would have to break his habit of no more than forty cuts. He hated going over the allotted cuts. It ruined everything for him, but he'd managed to bleed her out before he had to start a new ritual and he hated the thought she'd nearly ruined it for him.

It had taken him years to perfect the one he had now. He didn't want to start over and figure out what actions would keep the voice in his head silent. Searching for ways to satisfy the lust for blood and pain had been difficult to begin with, as he'd fought against the morals and ethics his father had taught, yet the hate and need in his soul had driven him to take the only way out he could. After the first time he'd killed, he'd found the release from the almost unbearable pressure euphoric and he'd become addicted to the violence.

The key jingled in the lock and he adjusted his gloves. It was time and his heartbeat settled, along with his nerves. He'd done this more times than he could count, perfecting his ritual along the way until in the moment of death, he'd achieved pure perfection with his victim. He froze when he heard her talking.

Had she brought someone home with her? He'd picked the day because it was in the middle of the week, and she never brought people home with her during the week. She was dedicated to her work and he admired that trait in her because he was the same way.

He waited to hear a responding voice, but there wasn't one. She must have been on her phone. He pushed the door to the pantry open a little, risking her seeing him to double-check. She stood at the counter, her back toward him, her hands waving as she talked. His upper lip curled in disgust. Again she was oblivious to his presence. No sense of self-preservation or even an instinct that something wasn't right in her house.

He couldn't take her while she was on the phone. No one could know she was gone until after he had her in the room. Once there, it wouldn't matter if someone reported her missing. No one would find her until he was done with her. Then he'd display her like the others and read about the police chasing their tails as they tried to find the Knife.

Snorting silently, he couldn't believe the media would give him such a pathetic nickname. No imagination these days. In the old days of newspapers, he would have gotten a much scary moniker, but he couldn't argue with them about it. It wasn't like he would be writing to the papers and complaining about what they called him. No, it was better to let them all stumble over each other while he laughed in the shadows.

She finished her phone call and tossed the phone on the counter as she started stripping out of her work clothes. He's stood in the pantry on other nights, getting a handle on her nightly routine so he could make his plans. He waited until he heard the shower come on upstairs, then he slid from the pantry and patted his pocket for the syringe.

He'd shoot her up with a tranquilizer before carrying her out of the back door wrapped in a sheet. A tall privacy fence surrounded her backyard, and it would be dark before he removed her from the house. Her neighbors weren't the nosy kind, plus none of them had dogs. He always had to worry about dogs because for some reason, they sensed the monster inside him and reacted angrily to it.

She wouldn't wake up until he had her confined and the game was ready to begin. He hoped she would be fun and fight, but not all of them had the heart of his last victim. Some of them gave up too easily and the creature living inside him would be very disappointed. To appease it, he had to butcher the body.

See, the newspapers reported he'd killed five women, but his count was far higher. The ones they'd found were the ones where everything had gone perfectly, where all the rituals had been completed to the monster's specifications. There were at least four other bodies he'd destroyed because something had happened, and the monster had demanded their entire annihilation. He'd made sure the police would never find those.

They were an embarrassment and a failure of his goal to be the best at what he did. He never wanted to see those victims again, and if he were ever caught, he would never mention them either. They deserved to be forgotten.

He crept up the stairs, calm and collected, ready for the ritual to begin again.

* * * *

Tanner opened the door when Macario knocked. Smiling, the agent reached out and grabbed the front of Macario's shirt, yanking him into the house. Before Macario could say anything, Tanner locked their lips together. Macario didn't protest. He simply encircled Tanner's waist with his arms and held him tight, taking the kiss deep and hot in seconds.

When his lungs burned and his brain begged for oxygen, he eased back, chest heaving. "Well, that was quite a greeting. I'm tempted to go back outside and see if you'll say hello like that again."

"Oh, I don't think you have worry about that. I'm willing to kiss you like that whenever you wish." Tanner winked and broke away from him. "Come on. I have dinner ready."

Macario hung his jacket and hat up on the rack beside the front door. He unclipped his gun and held it up. "Do you have some place I can put this?"

Tanner looked over his shoulder. "Just leave it on the table in the hall, or you can leave it in the living room. There aren't any kids around to play with it, so you'll be fine."

"Where do you keep yours?"

"I have one in the nightstand by my bed and my issued handgun is in a gun safe in the hall closet." Tanner waved a hand toward the door of his bedroom. "You can put yours in the nightstand with my other one."

"Thanks." Macario didn't like just leaving his gun lying around, even without children around.

He slid the gun in the drawer and returned to the kitchen where Tanner was dishing out spaghetti. Macario breathed deeply, his nose filling with the fragrant scents of tomato and garlic. "Did you make the sauce yourself?"

Tanner laughed. "Oh no. The one time I tried, I burnt it so badly I was traumatized. I've never tried it since then. It's much easier to get bottled sauce."

"It still smells good, and I really wouldn't have known the difference." He settled at the kitchen table when Tanner set the plate in front of him.

"Beer, soda or tea?" Tanner opened the refrigerator and asked.

"Beer." He took a bite of the pasta and moaned. "Christ, I don't care if it's homemade or not, this is damn good."

Tanner placed a bottle of beer beside Macario's plate, along with a tray of garlic cheese bread. After he took his place across from Macario, he dug in as well. They were quiet for a few minutes, taking the edge off their hunger. When the first couple of bites had eased the need, Macario met Tanner's gaze.

"You find anything in the evidence?"

Tanner frowned. "I'm not sure. I didn't get through all of it. Got called away for a consult on a different case. Once I'm done with every scene, I'll be able to figure out if there's anything there, or if I'm just talking out of my ass."

"If it's any help, you have a very nice ass." He laughed when Tanner blushed and tossed a piece of bread at him.

"Thank you, I guess." Tanner propped his chin on his hand and twirled pasta around his fork. "I still think I'm missing something. I can't figure out how he gets them out of wherever he grabs them without anyone seeing anything."

"We thought he might drug them, but there's never any drugs in their system and no needle marks where he might have pricked them." Macario leaned back in his chair, staring up at the ceiling.

"You know, you might be right. There are so many cuts

and wounds, how could you tell if there were any marks to indicate whether or not he drugged them. And if he did, maybe it wasn't with a needle. He could have slipped something in their coffee or food. Also, he keeps them long enough, the drug could have made its way out of their system by the time he dumps them." Tanner pursed his lips. "It would explain why no one ever saw a struggle."

Macario took a swig of beer then put the bottle on the table. "We'll go with the idea that he drugs them somehow, but it still doesn't tell us where he grabs them at. If it's at their house, they would have to know him well enough to allow him in."

"Or he could dress like a repair man or something like that."

"We checked with all the neighbors. No one remembers seeing a repair guy or anyone like that around in the days before the women disappeared." Macario finished his food then stood to carry the plate to the sink.

"See, that's the thing. No one really pays attention to repair trucks or delivery people. No one would think twice of something like that in the neighborhood."

"Speaking of which, that Suburban's back down the street again. I noticed it when I pulled into your driveway."

Tension suddenly filled the room and Macario looked up from where he stood, rinsing the plates before he put them in the dishwasher.

"Tanner?"

Chapter Eight

Fuck! Tanner didn't know what to say. How did he get Macario to ignore the Suburban without letting on he knew exactly whom those people in the vehicle were watching?

"Damn, I meant to tell them to move because they were getting noticeable," he muttered, hoping Macario would let it go.

"Tell who? Who are they? And what are they doing in your neighborhood?" Macario closed the dishwasher and turned it on. He wandered over to where Tanner stood. He slipped his arm around Tanner's waist and nuzzled his jaw. "What aren't you telling me?"

Tanner closed his eyes and nudged his panic down. He'd never thought this would be an issue, but he should have known once Macario started coming to his house more often, the man would notice anything out of the ordinary. Macario was a police officer, after all.

"They're there to keep an eye on me," he admitted.

Macario whirled him around and cupped his face in his hands. "Are you in danger?"

Tanner shook his head. "Not really. Just a precaution since I got a threat from the relative of a guy I testified against in a murder case last year. They're there to make sure nothing happens. It's been a week. I'm sure they'll get pulled soon."

He'd make sure they got pulled that night.

"You're sure it's nothing really serious? Where you should have protection twenty-four-seven?" Macario stared into Tanner's eyes. "I like you, Tanner, and I'd hate for anything to happen to you."

"Don't worry. I can take care of myself and, like I said,

they were just a precaution, but I think it'll be fine for them to leave."

Tanner kept his gaze on Macario's—no need to do anything to make Macario suspicious. Yet he'd told the truth as far as it went. The man's brother had threatened him and the Bureau had assigned protection for a few days until they'd decided the threat wasn't credible. Tanner just didn't mention the fact the Bureau had pulled his security escort yesterday.

"Okay. As long as you're sure you aren't in any danger." Macario frowned. "Why do you have a lily on your coffee table?"

Another question Tanner didn't really want to answer, but he bit the bullet. "I went to visit my mother's grave today and took lilies out for her. I ended up keeping one of them for here."

"Ah. Let's go sit in the living room and I'll catch you up on what I found out today."

"I have to use the bathroom first. I'll be right out."

He brushed his thumb over Macario's bottom lip and smiled before rushing to the bathroom. He made a short detour to his bedroom to grab his other phone. Leaning against the closed door, he flipped open his phone.

Call off your guys.

He pissed and washed his hands while waiting for a reply.

Problem?

Yes. Very Big Problem.

Done. Sorry.

TY.

Tanner tossed the phone in the top drawer of his dresser and changed into a pair of sweats and a T-shirt. Wandering out, he spotted Macario standing by the window, staring out into the street.

"Are we being attacked by zombies or something?"

Macario looked puzzled. "Why would we being attacked by zombies?"

"Most zombie movies have a scene where the humans are trapped in a house and one is always peering out the window looking for zombies." Tanner waved his hand. "Never mind. Why were you looking out the window?"

"The Suburban pulled off. I guess they figured you were safe." Macario gestured to the couch. "Let's see if anything I found out today will help you in the profiling."

"Fine with me." Tanner held up the new beer he grabbed. "You want another?"

"Sure."

They settled on the couch and Tanner took a long drink before looking at his lover. "Okay. I'm ready now."

Macario tilted his head and met Tanner's gaze. "Are you sure you're okay? You've gotten really tense after we finished eating."

Tanner reached out and threaded his fingers through Macario's hair. He brought their lips together and licked along the seam of Macario's mouth, begging for entrance. When Macario opened to him, he swept his tongue in to stroke along Macario's. He moaned as the man gripped his hips and pulled him closer. He straddled Macario's legs, never breaking their kiss. Tanner rocked into Macario's hips and they both groaned.

Pulling a few inches away, he rested his forehead against Macario's. "I'm sorry. I get a little weird after visiting my mother's grave. It upsets me, knowing I'm alone in the world."

"I can understand that," Macario murmured, placing a kiss on the tip of Tanner's nose. "Sorry if I made you uncomfortable or anything."

"No. You didn't. I'm just not used to dealing with anyone after one of my visits. Haven't really had a relationship where a guy hung around more than one time." He winced. "God, that makes me sound like a player."

Macario shook his head. "I never thought of it that way. I always thought of it as not being willing to play games and shit like that."

"Maybe." Tanner dropped his gaze to Macario's chest for a moment before looking into his dark eyes. "It might be this case as well, or the build-up from all the cases I've been working on lately. I haven't had a vacation since my mother died. I've been working non-stop. I'm sure a therapist would say it was to keep my mind off the fact she's gone."

"What do you say?"

Tanner lifted one shoulder. "I'd say they'd probably be right for the most part. I'm damn good at what I do, but it starts wearing on a man. All the shit humans do to each other."

He pushed to his feet and wandered over to the bookshelves. Staring at the pictures, he rubbed a thumb over the glass covering the photo of his high-school graduation where he poised with his mother.

"Are you thinking about quitting?"

Sighing, Tanner shook his head and looked at Macario. "Not at the moment. It's just in the back of my mind, the possibility exists I won't be doing this much longer."

"Why become a profiler in the first place if you don't like what you do?"

Tanner bit his lip. "Like I said, I'm good at what I do, and it made my mom proud."

"It made José cringe when he told his friends I became a policeman." Macario chuckled. "He didn't have a lot of trust in law enforcement. Maybe it came from the fact he started life as an illegal. I think he crossed the border as a drug mule."

"Might be true." Tanner placed his hand over his eyes for a moment as he rearranged his thoughts to focus on the serial killer case. "Okay. Did you learn anything new from the people at the gyms?"

Macario got his briefcase from where he'd dropped it in the entryway when Tanner had grabbed him. After setting it on the coffee table, he opened it and pulled out his notebook. Tanner watched him flip through the pages until he found what he was looking for.

"We talked to every person working at each gym. They all remembered the women, but they don't remember any of them having problems with any other member. We got the names and addresses of the people who weren't working today. We'll be talking to them tomorrow." Macario frowned. "I'm not sure the gym is where he finds them. It might just be a coincidence."

Tanner shook his head. "When you said two of them went to Tim's Gym, my instincts said that's where he finds them. Maybe he spotted them going into the gym and picked them in some way from that. There was no sign of forced entrance at any of the houses?"

"None. What? Do you think he somehow got their keys and let himself into their houses?" Macario rolled his eyes. "That seems a little far-fetched, doesn't it?"

"It does, but somehow he gets in their house."

He stalked over to where the photos were scattered all over the table. He clenched his hands to keep from sweeping them onto the floor. Frustration rocketed through him.

"He's out there stalking another one. He's going to take her to some deserted warehouse and kill her slowly and as painfully as possible. Maybe she ignored him when he tried to talk to her. Maybe she flirted with him and he hates women who are forward like that." Tanner closed his eyes, blocking out the horrific pictures of the dead women, but all he saw were their head shots, innocent and smiling before they crossed paths with the killer.

"They all colored their hair, maybe he didn't like women who tried to change what they truly looked like. Maybe that's why he picks them up at the gym." Macario joined him at the table.

Tanner wanted to say Macario's suggestion was

ridiculous, but he'd come across dumber reasons why people killed each other. If he could just figure out what connected them, why the killer chose them, he could help save another women. Yet nothing about them matched. Two were blonde and one brunette. The other two were red heads. They were all different heights and weights. The only thing they had in common were their sex and the fact they went to the gym.

"He doesn't like women," Tanner muttered.

"What was your first clue? The way he slices and dices them? Or the fact he carves something into their left breasts to defile them?"

"No. The carving isn't meant to defile them. It's his signature. Like any good artist, he signs his work. In a way, he sees them as paintings or sculptures. He carves the design for us to know it was his work." Tanner opened his eyes and traced one of the wounds. "He's done this before. I know there weren't any unsolved murders with this MO, but I guarantee you, he didn't just start killing four months ago."

Macario grunted. "If he's gotten away with killing before, why give us a chance to find the bodies now? Does he want to get caught?"

"That's not his reason behind leaving them where they'd be found. He's gotten arrogant. He believes he's untouchable and smarter than the police. Each time he kills and we don't gain any more clues, he begins to believe his own illusion of invincibility." He began to pace around the room, swerving to avoid Macario each time he came near the table. "He hates women, but I'm not sure it has anything to do with his childhood like most serial killers."

"Killing women to kill their mothers over and over again like they couldn't do as children."

"Right. He's intelligent, but I don't think he's college-educated. He probably didn't even graduate high school. In some way, he feels inferior to the women he kills. They're all college educated and work at high-powered jobs."

"Except for Marissa. She worked at a restaurant as a waitress," Macario pointed out.

"Yes, but that was just a recent job change. Before that she worked at the county courthouse, right?"

"Yeah."

"Maybe he started stalking her before she changed jobs. We don't really know how long he stalks them before he takes them. He might have made a list and picked them all before he ever killed the first one." Tanner grabbed a pen and his notebook from the table, scribbling the thought down. "I think it's one of the reasons he takes them—because they're smarter than him, or at least, society would see them as more successful and important than he is and he can't take that."

Macario tapped his fingers against his bottom lip and nodded. "You could be right. Add that to his profile and I'll make sure to let Billingsley know tomorrow. What kind of job do you think he has?"

"I'd usually say he probably had some blue collar type job, allowing him to spend time stalking the women without them noticing. Yet something's telling me he doesn't work anymore."

"Maybe that's what started him killing them. They're still working while he's out of a job." Macario jotted it down in his notebook.

Tanner shrugged. "It might have been that."

Macario bumped their hips together as he walked past. "I have to write up a short email to the major, letting him know what Sorensterm and I found out today. He'll expect me to brief him face-to-face tomorrow, but he'll also want something in writing."

"Go do it, and I want to check my email as well. I'm still waiting to hear back from some of those districts with those knife killings."

"But all those were drug related, and we know none of our victims had nothing to do with drugs."

Tanner couldn't explain why he wanted to see the crime

scenes photos from those drug executions. While he knew the women had nothing to do with drugs that they could find, he wasn't as positive about the killer. A person with such an affinity with knives didn't always fly under the radar. He could have been recruited at some point to work for the cartels as an enforcer.

It was far-fetched because the cartels didn't usually let their enforcers or workers moonlight doing other things, like murdering women for fun. The drug lords kept a tight grip on their people, ruling by fear and force. Yet what if one of the cartels let an enforcer go without taking him out permanently? It didn't make sense, but Tanner had seen stranger things happen.

He brought up his work email and checked the new messages. There were several from the different police departments he'd contacted. They were all sending copies of the complete files for their unsolved murders. He'd get them tomorrow, but some photos were attached and he opened them.

He cringed slightly when he saw the sheer brutality involved in the murders. One of the victims' necks had been sliced so deeply, his head was almost severed from his body. Blood covered everything in the vicinity of the body, unlike the scenes in Tanner's cases. If this was the same killer, had he gotten more sophisticated and fastidious about the blood? Or was his killing method simply evolving?

"Do you really think the perp who did this is our guy?" Macario spoke from right behind him.

Tanner jumped, not having heard Macario approach him. He relaxed into Macario's hands as his lover rubbed his shoulders. Tension slowly seeped away and he let his head drop forward.

"I'm not sure if he is or not, but we have to cover every avenue. Drug enforcers are serial killers, but usually they are caged or controlled by their bosses. So there doesn't tend to be any random killings outside of the drug world. The cartel bosses won't allow that. It lessens their power and ability to keep their people in line." Tanner shut down his computer. "Did you get your report typed up?"

"Yes." Macario scrubbed his bristling chin across Tanner's exposed neck. "I think we need to head to bed. There's nothing more we can do tonight."

Nodding, Tanner pushed to his feet to head toward his bedroom. He waited until Macario had stepped into the room before he shut the door and invaded the man's personal space. Macario leaned against the door and ran his hands over Tanner's head as Tanner dropped to his knees, fumbling with Macario's belt.

"I should be doing this for you. You need to relax more than I do," Macario muttered as Tanner undid his pants and pushed them down.

"I think this will be mutually beneficial." He winked up at the man.

"Well, I really wasn't about to stop you." Macario laughed.

Tanner let Macario brace his hand on his shoulder while he stepped out of his pants and underwear. He shoved them to the side and rocked back on his heels, eyeing the fat, hard cock standing proudly in front of him. He licked his lips as a drop of liquid welled up from the slit.

"Why don't you put your tongue to better use?"

He looked up at Macario and raised an eyebrow. "Did you really just say that?"

"What? Too porno-y for you?" Macario tried to look innocent.

Tanner trailed his finger down the length of Macario's cock while he thought. "Not really, just didn't think I'd ever hear you say something like that."

"Hey, I've watched plenty of pornos in my time." Macario's smile was crooked. "Of course, I admit I didn't watch them for the dialogue."

"Oh really? And what did you watch them for, Ranger Guzman?" He shrugged. "I think we can go without condoms this time."

Before Macario could answer him, Tanner opened and

swallowed Macario down to the base of his cock. He relaxed and Macario hit the back of his throat.

"Holy shit!" Macario's head banged against the door hard.

Tanner wanted to chuckle, but resisted the need. He slid a little bit of Macario's flesh out of his mouth and fisted it with his other hand. With everything where he wanted it, Tanner started giving Macario the best blow job he could. He used his tongue, his hand and his teeth a little, not wanting to hurt the man.

Macario grabbed his head roughly and Tanner moved his grip to Macario's hips. With a soft hum and a tap, he let Macario know it was okay to move. A grunt warned him of Macario's intentions. He braced and Macario began to move, stroking in and out with increasing speed. Trusting Macario not to knock him over, Tanner slid one of his hands from the man's hip to inside his own sweats to pump his cock.

He matched Macario's rhythm, gripping tight. His balls drew up to his body and a tingling pooled at the base of his spine. Tanner looked up at Macario and as their eyes met, his climax shot through him. Wet heat coated his hand while Macario thrust deep before freezing and flooding Tanner's mouth.

Tanner eased back slightly, leaving just the head of Macario's dick in his mouth, and he swallowed down what the man gave him. He milked both of their cocks, getting every drop of cum from each. When Macario collapsed against the door, Tanner licked the softened flesh before allowing it to slowly slide out of his mouth. He rested his forehead on Macario's hip and tried to catch his breath.

"Oh wow," Macario murmured, holding out his hand.

Tanner took it and let him pull him to his feet. They leaned on each other for a moment before Tanner stepped back and gestured toward the bathroom.

"Clean up and head to bed?"

Macario nodded and they went to the bathroom. Tanner

stripped and washed up while Macario watched him. After he'd finished, Macario reached out to cup his face. He met Macario's gaze with a questioning look of his own.

"Christ, I never thought I'd feel this way about anyone." Macario grimaced as he spoke.

Tanner's stomach dropped, and he nuzzled into Macario's hand. "Is that a good thing or a bad thing?"

Macario snorted and shook his head. "Damned if I know, Tanner. Like I said, I never wanted someone like I want you. I can't get through the day without thinking about you, and getting hard. It's a little embarrassing. Haven't had that happen since I was a teenager and any swift breeze would give me an erection."

"I guess that's a good thing, and I want to let you know, you're not alone in the hard-on department," Tanner admitted.

"Good. I didn't want to be the only one feeling this way." Macario placed a light kiss on his lips. "Let's get some sleep. Oh, and if you have a nightmare, wake me up. I could probably think of some way to help you get back to sleep."

Tanner grinned as Macario leered at him. He took the man's hand and led him back to bed. They climbed under the blankets and he wrapped his arms around Macario, pulling his lover's body tight against him.

"Night," he whispered into Macario's hair.

Macario patted his hip and muttered something Tanner couldn't make out. He closed his eyes and let the steady rhythm of Macario's breathing ease him into sleep.

* * * *

"He asked you to remove the men I put on him?"

Perez nodded. "Yes, sir."

"Why?"

"I believe it has to do with the man he's been seeing." He ducked his head, not sure how Victor would react to the knowledge that Tanner was sleeping with someone. That it was a man didn't matter, and would never matter to Victor. He'd always accepted who Tanner was.

After standing, Victor strolled over to the window, staring out into the dark garden. "Who is this man?"

"I think he's a Texas Ranger, sir. Our men have seen him at Tanner's house a few times in the last week, and he stays the night. They also followed Tanner to the man's apartment as well." He shrugged. "I'll do a background check on him."

"Do so. We don't want Tanner in trouble. He would tell me I worry too much about him, but he's my brother. I would take him to my compound in Mexico, if he'd allow me." Victor sighed. "He is too good to be tainted by all the blood we bathe in every day. Maybe it is best that he insists on being left alone."

"Yes, sir, I think you are right about that. Tanner would never survive in our world. I'll do the check and report back to you." Perez bowed then turned to leave the study.

"Wait."

He paused and turned back, meeting Victor's dark gaze. He searched for anger or any other emotion in the man's eyes he would need to deal with. It paid to be aware of how Victor was feeling. Nothing was there but concern. The slender man stepped closer, his hands tucked firmly in his pockets, yet that cool gaze trailed over his body and he shivered, just getting a glimpse of the heat that burned beneath the chill in Victor's eyes.

"Is there something else, sir?"

"The flowers?"

"Lilies, sir. I arranged for new ones to be sent every day." He pulled out his phone to scroll through the calendar section. "Would you like a different flower?"

"No, lilies are fine." Finally, Victor invaded his personal space and reached up to cradle his face. "You'll come to me?"

Like he would ever be able to say no to this man? It had nothing to do with the power over life and death he had over him. No, Perez would never deny Victor his body because he loved Victor Delarosa with every atom of his being.

Others feared Victor, and rightly so. There was no mercy in the man if he was cheated or someone he cared for was hurt. He would strike down a competitor without thinking, and in the cruelest way possible to send a message to the other cartels.

Yet Victor had never been anything but gentle with Perez, and Perez was the only one who had seen just how much Victor cared about his younger brother. The other men thought they watched Tanner because he was a dirty FBI agent and Victor might be able to use him at some point. So Victor wanted to know where Tanner was at all times.

None of them knew the family connection between Victor and Tanner, and Victor would kill to keep that secret. Perez knew because he'd seen it happen and he'd done it once himself. Perez's soul was pitch black from all the evil he'd done to keep Victor Delarosa alive. He understood he was going to hell, and he'd accepted his fate. None of it mattered as long as Victor continued to love him.

He nodded, wanting to feel those thin lips against his, but knowing he had to wait until everyone else was asleep. He wouldn't risk his boss's position by exposing their relationship. The men who ran the drug cartels were a macho group, and Victor sleeping with another man would be seen as a weakness—one his enemies would try to exploit. Perez would die before he became a liability for Victor.

"Good. I'll see you later then." His lover dropped his hand then stalked over to his desk. "Keep guys on Tanner, but tell them to make sure he and his lover don't notice them. I thought they were our best."

"They were, sir, but I don't think there's much they can do to keep him from discovering them. He is an officer of the law," he pointed out.

"They'd better not be spotted this time, or they'll be

dealing with me, and I know they would rather meet with you." Victor's smile was rather evil and Perez shivered.

"Of course, sir."

After leaving the study, Perez shut the door behind him. Taking a deep breath, he steadied his nerves. He hated how his boss affected him, and the two polar-opposite personalities residing in the man. Yet he understood why it all had to be that way. Hopefully the day would come when his boss could just be a man, not the monster everyone believed him to be.

Because Perez really did believe that Victor was a good man, but the life he'd been forced into by the choices of his parents had caused him to wall off the good inside him. He'd had to learn how to kill and not cry about it when he was young, so his father wouldn't beat him. Perez had been Victor's lover for a long time, and it was only in bed when they were truly alone that Victor could show the human side of himself.

As Victor Delarosa's lover, Perez was privy to a lot of the man's secrets, yet there were times when Perez would see a look on Victor's face that told him Delarosa held some so close to his heart that he'd never spill them. Perez vowed never to use those private moments to hurt Victor, but he also held them close to his heart as he prayed for the day they could leave this terrible drug world behind.

Straightening his shoulders, he went off to find the men who'd been watching Tanner. At least this time they would be given a second chance. If they failed and Tanner called them off again, he doubted the boss would be as forgiving.

Chapter Nine

She jerked awake, her eyes rolling in her head as she tried to figure out where she was. He stood in the shadows, watching and studying her. He rubbed his nose where she'd clipped him when he'd approached her while she was in the shower. Luckily, there wasn't any blood and she hadn't fought for long after he'd injected her. He'd carted her out of the house through the back door and had tossed her in the back of his truck.

The woman tugged on the chains holding her off the floor. He liked it when she struggled and cried out, begging for help, but like in space, there was no one around to hear her scream. He'd picked this kill room because the warehouse had been abandoned. He'd staked out the area, making sure the building was never used.

It wasn't and it had become his next base of operations. He never used the same place twice. It was too easy to grow lazy and believe no one would notice his activities. The more he came and went from the building, the more likely it was a homeless person would spy him and get curious. He couldn't risk that happening.

She yanked and kicked, though the chains around her ankles and wrists wouldn't allow her much movement.

"Where are you, you son of a bitch? I know you're around here somewhere."

He rolled his eyes at her shouts. Taunting him wouldn't drive him to move before he was ready. He shifted and the rustling of his clothes alerted her to where he stood.

"Why won't you let me see you? Are you the one who killed those other women?" She turned her gaze on him the best she could. "Do you want me to scream and plead for you not to hurt me? Do you get off on my fear?"

Snorting silently, he shook his head. Did they all believe the killing was sexual in nature? He'd never touched one of them in that way. He shuddered at the thought of having any carnal knowledge of the women he killed. God made whores for that. He wanted nothing to do with women who believed they were smarter than him, as she proved while she ranted at him.

He leaned against the rough brick wall while she called him names and tried to psychoanalyze him. When she ran out of energy and her voice grew hoarse, he reached down and pulled his knife from its sheath. Stepping out of the shadows, he stalked toward her, letting the low light of the candles reflect of the surface of the blade.

"You think you know me because you read the newspaper. You think you're better than me because you have a job and a college education. Did all your classes teach you how to react when a man cuts you? Do you know how to free yourself when you're chained to a wall at his mercy?" He sneered at her. "Stupid *puta*!" He spat at her feet. "I followed you for days and you never once noticed me. I stole your keys and you never even figured it out, just thought you lost them somewhere. You were so happy when you realized you just left them at home one day."

Her eyes widened as he regaled her with her routine throughout the day. The fear she'd hidden earlier behind her brave words slowly blossomed in her face and he grinned, striking quickly like a snake. The first thin line of blood trickled down her face from where he'd cut her cheek.

"By the time I am finished with you, you'll be excited for death. You will welcome it with open arms as your blood pools at your feet. With each cut, you will understand that I am the one in power, not you. I am the one who is smarter and I'm the one who gets to say whether you live or die." He shrugged and wiggled the knife. "Of course, we both know you'll die. I can't leave you alive now that you've seen my face."

Reaching into his pocket, he pulled out his earphones. Usually, he liked to listen as they pleaded with him for their lives, but not this one. He hated her nasally voice and the way everything came out as an order. He would listen to his favorite music while he bled her dry.

* * * *

Their phones rang at the same time, and both Macario and Tanner sat up in bed, reaching for them. Tanner rolled out of bed and grabbed his work phone first, heading straight to the closet while he answered.

"Wallace."

Macario checked the ID and answered, "Where's the body, Sorensterm?"

"I'll text you the address. It's still rather fresh. He didn't wait for the usual twelve hours before he dumped this one."

He found his underwear and managed to get them on while still listening to Sorensterm. "I'll be there as soon as I can."

"Make sure that profiler comes as well. He might get something from this scene since it's really fresh."

"Okay."

Hanging up, he snatched his shirt off the floor and frowned at the wrinkles in it.

"Here, wear one of my suits. We're the same size and no one will know." Tanner held out a charcoal gray suit. "Besides, it'll match your hat."

Macario took it and grimaced at Tanner. "We don't have time to worry about whether my hat matches my clothes."

"No, we don't," Tanner agreed.

They got dressed without getting in each other's way. Macario gathered the files and his laptop before stuffing them into his briefcase. With his gun settled in its familiar spot on his hip, and his badge clipped to his belt, Macario raced out of Tanner's house. Tanner locked the door and followed him down the front walk.

"I'll meet you there." Tanner waved at him before getting in his car.

Nodding, Macario climbed into his. A brief thought crossed his mind about what Sorensterm might say with the two of them showing up at the scene at the same time, but he found he didn't care whether his some-time partner figured out that he and Tanner had slept together. At the moment, all he cared about was finding the bastard who was killing women in Houston.

He punched in the address Sorensterm had texted him into his GPS and took off. Tanner pulled out right behind him, but Macario lost him in the early morning traffic. Twenty minutes later, he parked his car in front of another abandoned warehouse. Police cars were angled to block off the street while uniformed officers put up crime scene tape and kept the gawkers from seeing anything.

As he approached the opened door, he heard another car arrive. Sorensterm stepped out of the warehouse and they watched Tanner climb out of his vehicle. The agent reached in and pulled out a carrier holding three large coffees from the local fast food place.

"Sorry. I stopped for coffee. Figured none of us had a chance to drink some before this." Tanner held out the cups for Macario and Sorensterm to take.

Sorensterm met Tanner's gaze. "You can drink coffee, knowing what you're going to walk into here?"

"What are we walking into? This isn't the kill site, is it? It's just the dump site." Tanner took a sip of his coffee.

"Yes, but still it's not a pretty sight." Sorensterm eyed him.

Macario snorted. "When are any murder scenes a pretty sight? This isn't the first crime scene Agent Wallace has seen, Sorensterm. You're drinking coffee as well, and you've actually seen the victim. Don't harass him."

Sorensterm looked at Macario with a raised eyebrow, but

kept his mouth shut. Macario gestured to the building.

"Who called it in?"

"Don't know. Another anonymous call came into dispatch. More than likely, it was some homeless person who ducked into the warehouse for shelter and found it. Thank God, they found her shortly after he dumped her or this would be really bad." Sorensterm led the way into the warehouse.

Macario gritted his teeth and silently agreed with his partner. He'd been sent to murders where the victim hadn't been found for days. The stench and appearance, at times, were enough to even make him sick. Yet having a fresh site could be good for them because they might be able to get some clues that could have disappeared over time.

There were several uniformed police milling around while the crime scene techs got ready to go in.

"Have we considered the fact that the perp might be the one calling in these anonymous tips?" Tanner said quietly as he walked beside him.

"I've been thinking that myself. Just haven't said it out loud yet. But you're probably right. It seems rather convenient that we get these calls when we do."

Tanner nodded. "So he wants us to find his victims, and is making sure we do so in a reasonable amount of time."

"No one's been in except the person who found her and the uniform who responded to the call. When he got here, he looked in, saw her, and backed out. He called us right away." Sorensterm nodded toward one of the younger cops.

"Make sure someone talks to him about what he saw. Never know when it might be important." Macario grabbed a pair of gloves and booties from the techs and slipped them on. He set his coffee down before he entered the room. Stopping just outside the scene, he took a deep breath.

A gentle and quick touch to his back told him Tanner stood close to him. Macario never thought he'd care whether the guy he fucked understood what he dealt with every day. Yet knowing Tanner not only understood but dealt with the same shit in his job as Macario did, brought a surge of emotion he'd never really felt before. Maybe it was contentment or an odd sort of happiness. He shook his head. Now wasn't the time to think about it.

They stepped inside the room and Macario narrowed his eyes. Something was different about this killing.

"He didn't finish the ritual," Tanner murmured as they stood inside the door.

Macario nodded, stepping up to where the body sprawled in a haphazard pentagram shape, except her legs weren't spread toward the corners. He rubbed his hand over his mouth, swallowing the anger until it burned in the pit of his stomach.

"Yet he had time to carve the design into her chest." Tanner pointed toward the woman's left breast. "It proves the pentagram isn't an important part of his ritual. He can do what he needs to do to satisfy his urges while not finishing it."

Macario turned in a slow circle, his eyes searching every nook and cranny of the room. Aside from not finishing the star, there was something else different about the scene. He spied a pile of debris in the corner. He walked over and crouched down beside it. It looked like a blanket.

"Tanner. Sorensterm. Come here," he called over his shoulder to the other two.

They joined him and stared down at the fabric.

"Does that look like a blanket?"

"Yes." Tanner turned and gestured to one of the techs. "Come and take a picture of this before we touch it."

"Yes, sir." The tech scurried over to where they gathered. She snapped pictures and wrote down all the information they had from just looking at it. She labeled an evidence bag before handing it to Tanner. "Here you go, Agent."

"Thank you." He waved her away and met Macario's gaze. "It's your case, Ranger. Go ahead."

Macario rolled his eyes, but pulling his pen out of his

pocket, he poked the blanket. Nothing moved and he took a deep breath before pinching the edge between his fingers. He tugged it, slowly unfolding it from where it had been thrown.

"Do you think it was used to transport the body or is it some squatter's?" Sorensterm wrinkled his nose at the smell. "It certainly smells like a homeless person's been using it."

Breathing through his mouth, Macario spread it out and they looked at it. While he stood, Tanner crouched down and pointed to several stains on the fabric.

"Those look like blood stains and not urine marks. This fabric is high quality, and it's not torn anywhere. This didn't come from a shelter or a thrift store. If you check, I'm sure you'll find it available at some of the higher end department stores." Tanner coughed slightly. "It probably came with her."

"Is it our killer's?" Macario made a note about sending someone out to check on what Tanner had said.

Tanner pushed to his feet and frowned. "No. He isn't going to be buying nice things at expensive stores, especially if he's going to wrap a body in it. I think if you check the victim's house, you'll find a matching sheet set or something."

"He took her from her home? Is that what you're saying?" Excitement surged through Macario.

Tanner shrugged and tucked his hands in his pockets. "It's possible. I'm not saying it's for sure or anything. You'll be able to confirm it when you figure out who she is and send people around to her place."

Macario clenched his jaw, but didn't give into the urge to shake Tanner hard. The agent wouldn't commit to anything unless he was absolutely sure of what he said. Of course, a lot of what Tanner did came from instinct, though he had a lot of experience with other serial killers to base his theories on.

"Do you think he took all of them from their homes?"

Macario held up his hand to keep Tanner from hedging. "I should have said, what does your instinct tell you about how he gets them?"

Tanner hunched slightly, his eyes focused on the floor around the body. "Everything in my gut says he takes them from their homes. I would bet money on the fact he probably drugs them somehow and carries them out. I didn't get to check out where all the victims live, but I'm guessing they live in places where their neighbors don't really pay much attention to what goes on around the neighborhood. Also, some of them might have privacy fences or something to make it easy for him to get them out without anyone noticing anything odd."

Macario thought about the houses he checked out and remembered only two of them with fenced backyards. Didn't mean Tanner was wrong though. Macario's gaze landed on Tanner when the agent stiffened. They'd moved closer to the body while the techs gathered evidence from around the edges of the room.

"What?" He tapped his pen against Tanner's biceps. "Do you see something?"

"She died too quickly." Tanner pointed to the slices covering her body. "There aren't enough slices here for him to have fulfilled his need. Her throat wound isn't deep enough to be the killing blow. She was dead before he even thought about cutting her throat."

Sorensterm shifted while Macario jotted down what Tanner had said, making a note to double-check with the ME.

"What could have caused that? Wouldn't he have noticed she was losing a lot more blood than they normally do?"

Tanner shot Sorensterm a puzzled look. "He's not a doctor. His ritual ensures they're usually unconscious by the thirtieth cut. He really wouldn't notice if they were bleeding too much or too fast. Caught up in the ritual of cutting them and the blood already coating him, he would never catch on to the fact she was bleeding too much until it was too late."

"What does that mean?" Macario was afraid he knew what Tanner was going to say.

"He's going to grab a new victim within the next two days or so and try to make sure his ritual is done right this time."

"Fuck!" Sorensterm growled. "He's escalating that fast?"

"Yes, but the other issue is his need for killing wasn't completely fed with this murder." Tanner waved a hand to encompass the entire room. "Something about this woman ruined it for him. He's already picked out his next victim and probably planned out how he's going to take her as well. There's no such thing as spontaneity with this man. I wouldn't be surprised to find out he plotted out which women he'd take before he even killed the first one."

Macario stood beside the woman and stared at the floor. He couldn't look into her empty eyes, knowing he let her down by not finding the bastard who killed her before she'd been taken. More guilt piled upon the mound he already had concerning Marissa. Something glittered when one of the camera flashes went off.

After pulling out his penlight, he dropped to a knee and turned it on, directing the beam toward the item on the floor. A key glistened in the light and Macario's pulse sped up.

"I've got something here," he called to one of the techs.

"What did you find?" Tanner and Sorensterm joined him.

"I got a key. It's clean and looks new, so I'm thinking it wasn't here when he dumped the body." He moved out of the way so the tech could take a picture of the item before he picked it up and slid it in an evidence bag.

"Try her door with it," Tanner suggested.

"Why would he have her keys on him?" Macario rocked back and looked up at Tanner.

Tanner shook his head and wandered out of the room, his head lowered and a thoughtful look on his face. Sorensterm glanced at him with a questioning expression.

"Where's he going?"

Macario shrugged. "Don't know. I'm sure he won't be far if we need to talk to him."

Tanner poked his head back in. "I need close-up photos of that carving in the victim's chest. I need it from every angle, especially an above shot."

"Yes, Agent Wallace."

"Thank you. Once you get back, make sure you send those particular pictures to me right away." Tanner glanced over at Macario. "I'm going to head back to my office. We'll meet up later this afternoon and compile all the information we have."

"Fine." Macario waved him out of the room.

"Why's he heading out? Seems to me he should be hanging around and looking over things here. He might learn something new about this guy." Sorensterm curled his lip.

Macario stared after Tanner for a second before turning away to watch the techs processing the scene. "I think he's seen all he needs to see here. I'm sure those pictures are more important to him than to us."

"I don't remember. Why does he think those carvings are important?"

"He believes the carving is the true ritual. The display is a secondary and not very important part." Macario gestured toward the awkward placement of the body. "It's why the killer can dump her without finishing it and not have any problem. She might have died too fast, but he did the carving like he wanted. Also, Agent Wallace believes there's something wound inside the carving and it's a clue to the identity of the bastard who did this."

Sorensterm shot him a look. "Seriously?"

"Yes. So we'll do our job and let him do his." Macario pushed to his feet and headed out of the warehouse. "Let's go canvas the area. We'll get some of the uniforms to help us."

* * * *

"Were you able to see if that key fit the victim's house?"

Macario looked up to see Tanner leaning against the doorframe, hands stuffed in his jeans pockets with a folder tucked under his arm. He let a small smile crack his face as he eyed the bulge at the man's groin.

"You were right. Is that what you wanted to hear?" He rocked back in his chair, fingers threaded and resting on the back of his neck.

"It's always good to hear that." Tanner entered the conference room and looked around. "This is the task force room?"

"Yeah." Macario shrugged. "Guess they figured we needed a spot to hang the pictures and store all the evidence."

"Good." Tanner tossed the folder on the table in front of Macario. "You can hang those up as well."

"What are they?" Macario reached out and opened the folder, shuffling through the photos. "Are these the photos you enlarged of the carvings?"

"Yes."

After standing, Macario joined Tanner in front of the dry-erase board where all the headshots of the victims hung. He attached the photograph of the sixth victim, Leslie Barnharm. He bumped hips with Tanner as he turned away.

Tanner touched his arm and he stopped. Meeting Tanner's gaze, he raised an eyebrow in a silent question.

"Don't beat yourself up about this, Macario. There's no way you would have been able to stop this from happening. We're getting there though, and we'll catch him." Tanner looked like he wanted to kiss Macario, but he didn't give in. "Your task force will find him. My gut's saying you'll do it before another woman dies."

"Thanks for having confidence in me." Macario brushed his fingers over Tanner's hand. "Were you able to figure anything else out after seeing the pictures of the newest carving?"

"Not yet, but I got called in for a consultation on another

case. I haven't had a chance to look them over. I plan on doing that as soon as this briefing is over."

"Oh shit, I forgot about that." Macario went back and dropped into his chair, bringing his report back up on his computer screen. "I have to finish typing up my notes before everyone gets here."

"I'm going to get a cup of tea while you do that. I don't want to get you in trouble with Major Billingsley. I just wanted to give you those."

Macario waved as Tanner strolled out of the room while typing with one finger to fill out his report. His frustration grew while he read about no one noticing anything strange around Leslie's house. They'd found her shower curtain torn off the rod in the bathroom, but that was the only sign of a possible struggle. A plastic cap that might have belonged to a syringe was found behind the toilet like it had been kicked there during a fight, so Tanner's idea of the man drugging his victims was proving to be right.

More and more clues were appearing as the case went on, but Macario didn't want to run the risk of another woman dying while they tried to figure shit out. They needed a witness to see a stranger in a place he shouldn't be. They needed a face to put out in front of the public to see if they could get suspects. So far, nothing had come of canvassing the neighborhoods, because it appeared he took them at night when others slept.

"Mac, tell me you've gotten something on this son of a bitch. I want a face or a name or something." Billingsley charged into the conference room, followed by the other members of the task force. Tanner brought up the rear, sipping on his tea and bracing his shoulder against the back wall.

"Well, sir, we're getting closer and I think it'll break soon. I'm sure someone saw something and we'll keep talking to people until we get a witness." Macario stood up and moved to the front of the room. "I will say we figured out how he kidnapped the women. At least, we're pretty sure we know how. We found a key at the dumpsite and it fit Leslie Barnharm's lock. It was new. Somehow he gets a hold of their keys and makes a copy of them."

Billingsley nodded, but didn't look entirely happy with that information. "What else?"

"He drugs them. At the latest victim's house, we found a torn shower curtain and a plastic cap. I gave it to the lab to check and see if there's any trace of drugs on it. He drugs his victims and carries them out wrapped in something he finds at the house. It happens in the middle of the night when the neighbors are sleeping, so there aren't any usual witnesses."

Macario stuffed his hands in his pockets and paced before everyone. "We've done our initial canvas and nothing's come of it, but we'll continue to ask questions and I'm sure we'll find something. He's getting more arrogant and sloppy."

"Okay, now go over everything again." Billingsley settled back in his chair.

Macario sighed silently, but got ready to go over everything they knew. Movement at the back of the room caught his attention, and he watched Tanner slip from the meeting. Frowning, he made a mental note to find Tanner and see what was so important the man had had to leave.

* * * *

After returning to the federal building, Tanner dashed into his office then started opening the envelopes that had been delivered while he was at the Rangers' headquarters. He'd gotten a text from the receptionist that the photos and files he'd requested had arrived. He wanted to see the photos from the drug murder scenes. Something had been nagging him since he'd started studying those carvings.

He dumped out all the photos and set the envelopes aside. It didn't really matter where each set of photos came from. He wasn't trying to solve their cases, though if he figured out the drug killer was the serial killer, he would let them all know.

There was a note attached to one group of pictures.

Agent Wallace, we believe these two killings are to be laid at the feet of the Delarosa cartel. Juan Mencia is one of Delarosa's enforcers and one of the more dangerous ones at that. If he's your killer, be careful when you go after him. Delarosa isn't known for allowing his men to be taken by the police.

"Fuck." Tanner kept his voice low, even though there wasn't anyone near him.

Usually an enforcer for one of the cartels would be considered a serial killer, but he only focused on people the cartels wanted dead or made an example of. Rarely did they branch out into killing people not involved in the drug trade. The heads of the cartels kept a tight grip on their people, and most would never think about going against their boss.

If Juan Mencia was really to blame for the killings, then either Delarosa wasn't aware of what his man was doing, or Mencia had been cut loose from the cartel. The possibility could explain the impression of arrogance Tanner had gleaned from the crime scene. The Rangers would have to make sure all their evidence was perfect before they went after someone connected to the cartels. Tanner shook his head and started to look at the photos.

Losing himself in the different crime scene photos, Tanner marked similarities and differences between the drug killings and the Houston victims. Several he marked for further examination, and he decided to call the lieutenant who had written the note.

"What was so important you had to rush out of the briefing?"

Tanner glanced up to see Macario standing in the doorway of his office, bracing a shoulder against the doorframe.

"These." He gestured to the photos scattered over his

desk.

Macario strolled over to him and picked up one of the photos. "You asked for the drug killing photos. Why?"

"I wanted to definitely cross them off as possibly being connected. Even if the women had no connection to drugs that we know of, we have to make sure we don't overlook any lead." Tanner met Macario's narrowed gaze. "I didn't go behind your back or anything. I just decided that this stuff would help me work up a better profile."

His lover frowned, but Tanner got the feeling Macario's issue wasn't with Tanner looking at the drug photos. He studied Macario as he wandered around Tanner's office, hands stuffed in his pockets.

"What's wrong?" He leaned back in his chair and put his feet up on his desk.

"Why do you think something's wrong?" Macario swung around, but didn't look at him.

"You don't strike me as the type of guy who paces very often, yet you've been circling my office like an expectant father."

Macario rolled his eyes. "Mr. Levisten left me a message. Marissa's funeral is the day after tomorrow. I'm trying to decide whether I should go or not."

Tanner dropped his feet to the floor then stood. He shut and locked his office door before approaching Macario. After reaching out, he cupped the back of Macario's head to bring their mouths together. Tension stiffened Macario for a second, but Tanner didn't let him move away.

He swiped his tongue into Macario's mouth, teasing and daring his lover to participate. He smiled mentally when Macario threaded his fingers through Tanner's hair and took the kiss deeper. Tanner didn't let it go too far because they couldn't do anything while at the office.

After a minute or two, Tanner stepped back, breaking the kiss. He rubbed his thumb over Macario's bottom lip. "You do what you feel is right. If you want to go to her funeral, I'll go with you."

"You would?"

Tanner nodded. "Sure. We're dating, sort of, aren't we? And even if we weren't sleeping together, I'd still go with you because you're my friend, Macario."

Macario blinked and seemed a little surprised, making Tanner wonder if Macario had many close friends. Tanner walked over to his desk and rested a hip on the edge.

"I thought you and Sorensterm were friends outside of work. You play poker together, don't you?"

"Yeah, but I don't tell him personal things. None of the guys I play cards with are what I'd consider close friends. Certainly, I wouldn't feel comfortable asking any of them to come to a funeral with me." Macario paced. "Do you have any close friends?"

Tanner shook his head. "Not really. Like I said, it was always just my mom and I."

Plus if any hint of his past got out, he would be in big trouble. A stray thought entered his mind and Tanner found himself wondering for the first time how he'd managed to get his job at the Bureau with his background. Something should have red flagged him. When he asked his mother before applying to the Bureau, she'd said not to worry and he hadn't, but now he started to think about it.

Had his father pulled strings or paid the way for Tanner to get this job? What would happen if Macario ever found out about Tanner's family?

"Well, it must have been lonely," Macario murmured as he wandered around the room.

"Yeah. It was, but until Mama died, I never realized it. Now that she's gone, I think about it a lot." Tanner shrugged when Macario looked at him. "Of course, it could be simply that I'm getting older and don't want to be alone all my life."

"We're not that old." Macario grimaced and shook himself like he wanted to get rid of the bad thoughts. "I have to get back to the office and grab Sorensterm. We're heading out to interview some more people. Maybe we'll get something."

Chapter Ten

Tanner left his gun and badge at home, taking great pains to ensure he didn't look like a cop. After flagging down a cab, he gave the driver the address and settled back for the ride.

What would Macario do if he found out the truth about Tanner's family? Tanner ran his hand over his hair and heaved a mental sigh. At the moment, all he could do was hope his lover didn't discover anything until after the case was solved.

The cab pulled up in front of the large ornate iron gates. Tanner climbed out and paid the driver before heading to the intercom. He pressed the buzzer.

"Yes?"

"I'm here to see Perez."

"Do you have an appointment?"

"No, but if you'd tell him Pablo wishes to speak to him, I'm sure he'll find time for me."

"Pablo, huh?"

"Yes."

The intercom went silent, and Tanner stuffed his hands in his pockets. He made sure to face the security camera mounted on the fence to one side of the gate. Hiding his face wouldn't help get him in, though once Perez heard who wanted to see him, he'd be ushered in quickly.

"An escort will be down in a second."

The gate unlocked and slid open far enough for Tanner to slip through. He stayed just on the other side, not interested in roaming the grounds. A golf cart sped up to him and the cold-eyed man driving nodded for him to get in. Tanner did without question and they headed up to the big house.

Two armed guards escorted him into a room where another grim-faced man patted him down. Tanner didn't protest, understanding why such precautions were necessary.

"Pablo, what the hell are you doing?" Perez stalked into the room and backhanded Tanner.

His lip split and while every muscle in Tanner's body yelled at him to strike back, he didn't. Appearances needed to be kept and he needed to talk to Perez.

"I'm sorry, Perez," he whined. "My wife had a list of shit she wanted me to do. The bitch wouldn't get off my ass until I finished them."

"Mr. Delarosa doesn't like to be kept waiting. Remember that because next time my greeting won't be as friendly."

"Yes, sir." He whimpered, hanging his head submissively.

"Come with me. We must discuss what Mr. Delarosa wishes you to do for him."

Perez turned sharply and strolled out of the room with Tanner following meekly behind. Tanner kept his gaze squarely on Perez's back. He didn't want to see anything law enforcement might be interested in.

"Step in here and wait. Mr. Delarosa will be with you in a minute."

As Tanner walked past him into the room, Perez whispered, "There is water and napkins for your lip on the side bar."

"Thank you," Tanner muttered.

Perez shut the door with a snap and Tanner searched out the supplies to clean up his lip. He didn't have to wait very long before another door opened and Victor Delarosa stepped in. Victor frowned when he saw Tanner's injury.

"What happened?"

"No big deal. Perez had to keep up appearances."

"He hit you?"

The growl in Victor's voice didn't bode well for Perez.

"I'm okay, Victor. We have more important things to

discuss."

Victor didn't look convinced and Tanner hoped he wouldn't punish Perez.

"I need your help."

"Ah, *hermano*, I'll give you any help I can."

Tanner grinned at his older brother. "I know, and that's why I'm here. Oh, I wanted to tell you I liked the new tombstone you had made for Mama."

He gasped as Victor swept him into a hard hug. He embraced Victor back, hating the choices made in the past.

"She deserves the best, Pablo. She wouldn't accept anything while she was alive. She can't complain now."

"True."

Victor motioned to two leather chairs. "Sit. Let us discuss what help I can give you. Would you like something to drink?"

Tanner shook his head. "No, thank you. Victor, have you seen Juan lately?"

"Juan?" Victor's brow furrowed in thought while he poured himself a highball of whiskey. "I don't believe so, but I never liked him, so Perez had more contact with him."

"Could you ask Perez when he last spoke to him?"

"Certainly." Victor picked up a phone then called Perez, asking him to come to the study. After setting the receiver down, Victor eyed Tanner.

"Why are you asking about one of my enforcers?"

Tanner pulled a flash drive from his pocket. "I think he's involved in a series of murders around Houston."

"Murders?" Victor looked puzzled. "I haven't asked him to do any work for me lately."

"And if these were drug-related, you know I wouldn't be here."

"That is true, *mi hermano*." Victor conceded the fact with a nod of his head. He took the flash drive Tanner held out to him.

"What is this?"

"Crime scene photos. There have been six murders in the

last five months. All women. All killed with a knife before being displayed."

His older brother scowled with disgust. "What makes you believe Juan is involved?"

"Not just involved. I believe he is the killer. What little I know about him, mostly information gathered by law enforcement, he's good with a knife, hates women and is a total psychopath."

No argument seemed forthcoming.

"Besides when I reviewed the crime scene photos, I spotted something that convinced me he was the killer."

When a knock sounded on the hallway door, Victor gave permission to enter. Perez joined them, heading right to Tanner and lifting his chin to look at the cut.

"I'm sorry, Pablo."

Smiling, Tanner shook his head. "I've had worse done to me, Perez. It's no big deal."

"We'll talk about that later," Victor informed Perez. "Right now, Pablo has something to ask you."

Tanner winced slightly, knowing that conversation wasn't one he wanted to be a part of. Victor tended to be protective of Tanner and punished any who hurt him, even Perez, who had been his brother's right-hand man for decades.

"Yes, boss." Perez bowed. "How can I be of service?"

"When did you last talk to Juan Mencia?"

Perez looked puzzled. "Why are you asking about him? He isn't giving you any trouble, is he? I swear he doesn't know who you are."

"I think he's a serial killer," Tanner said as bluntly as possible.

"Truly?"

"Yes."

While Perez pursed his lips and nodded, Victor opened the file of photos to study them.

"You think he's the one the newspapers call The Knife."

Tanner sat in one of the chairs. "I do."

"What about the police? Obviously the FBI is involved

since you are here, but are the Rangers part of the investigation?" Perez asked, hands propped on his hips.

Victor motioned for Perez to come and look at the pictures. As Perez did so, Victor poured himself another drink and sat across from Tanner.

"It's a joint task force and the Rangers have the lead on the case," Tanner told them.

"Then why come to me and risk everything if they find out we're related?"

Tanner thought about Macario and how every day, his lover was more and more eaten up with guilt. Macario was losing hope that his sister's murderer would be found and Tanner feared that he'd lose Macario if the murderer was never found.

"I don't care about my job. I never really have, but someone I care about lost his foster sister to the killer and I want to bring him some justice."

"Someone you care about, hmmm? Would that be the Ranger your superiors paired you with?"

His cheeks heated and Tanner ducked his head. Victor had never cared who Tanner slept with. He'd often told Tanner that. Tanner had decided several years ago that if Victor himself wasn't gay, he was at least bi. Victor often surrounded himself with beautiful women, but his relationship with Perez ran deep and loving, even when Perez did something Victor didn't like.

He rarely spent any time with his brother, since both of them were afraid someone would spot them together, but the time he did spend, he noticed the connection between Victor and Perez. It wasn't simply the bond between an employer and his employee. Their bond went deeper, like lover to lover. Tanner hoped they loved each other. For all that his brother was a cartel kingpin and a murderer, Tanner wanted him to be happy, because he saw how destroyed Victor was from living the life he'd been forced into.

"Yes." Tanner saw no reason to lie. More than likely his brother knew everything about Macario already.

"Ah, good. I'm glad you have someone," Victor murmured.

"I talked to Juan six months ago when I informed him that Mr. Delarosa no longer required his services." Perez stood next to Victor's chair, holding the flash drive out for Tanner to take.

"Now it would appear disposing of him would have been best for everyone," Victor commented.

"Juan killed those women. The *J* carved in their flesh above the left breast is his trademark." Perez looked pale under his golden tan.

As ruthless and cold-blooded as Victor and Perez could be, they didn't believe in killing innocents. Tanner's brother impressed enough fear and respect with his personality alone, he had no need to kill women or children.

In many ways, Victor was the devil incarnate, yet he had his own set of morals.

It was those morals that kept Tanner believing his brother was still worth saving. Those and the way Victor treated him. Of course, even the most evil of men have done good things in their time. Every person, good or bad, has a gray spot in his or her soul.

"I spotted that." Tanner stuck the drive in his pocket.

"Why did you come to see me if you already knew this?" Victor stared at him.

"I wondered if you might know where he's hiding. If his pattern holds true, he'll kill again within the next day or so." Tanner pushed to his feet to pace. "He doesn't kill them right away. Juan kidnaps them, plays with them a day or two before killing them and dumping the body. We need to know where he takes them."

Victor and Perez shared a long glance between them. When Victor nodded, Perez left.

"Go back home, Pablo. We will get you your information. I do want to reassure you that I had nothing to do with these murders. These women weren't involved in any of my business, and besides, you know I don't condone the killing of women."

Tanner believed him as Victor embraced him. He encircled his brother's waist and hugged him back.

"Juan getting caught won't harm you, will it?"

Tanner knew it would only be a matter of time before the DEA or the *Federales* took his brother down, but he didn't want it to be because he'd asked Victor for help.

"Don't worry about me, *hermano*. I have my ways of ensuring I won't be harmed by Juan's arrest. You must get this killer off the street and I'll help you." Victor's smile was sad as he gestured toward the door. "Now go back home and try to forget you have an older brother."

After nodding, Tanner left, not looking at any of Victor's other men. He kept his head down, acting cowed from his meeting with the boss.

There was a cab waiting for him at the end of the driveway. He told the driver to take him to the downtown library. Tanner didn't want anyone connecting him with Victor. After climbing out of the cab, he pulled out his phone and called Macario.

"Guzman."

"Macario. How's your day going?" He smiled at the gruffness of his lover's voice.

"I'm better now that I'm hearing from you. Did you do what you needed today?"

"Yeah. You want to meet me for dinner? I'm downtown by the library."

"Sure. I'm ready to quit for the day. I'll meet you at Jones's in about thirty minutes."

"See you soon."

After hanging up, he stuffed the phone in his pocket, and strolled toward Jones's. As he walked, he thought.

Should he say something to Macario about going to Victor and asking him for information about Juan? Would Macario understand the complexity of Tanner's life?

No, he'd wait until after Juan was caught and sentenced. He didn't want to risk everything. He'd always been as honest as possible, but sometimes omitting things was better than spilling everything.

He went into Jones's and sat at the bar, waiting for Macario to join him. He sipped his beer and let go of his worries. Victor would get him what he needed and Macario and the others would take Juan down. He'd done his job.

A hand brushed his shoulder and he turned to smile at Macario. He winced slightly at the pull on his split lip.

"What happened?" Macario growled, his hands clenched tight.

Tanner knew his lover wanted to touch him, but it was another risk neither of them wanted to take.

"Don't worry. Just a slight issue, and it's my only injury." He grabbed his beer after tossing some money on the bar to pay for it. "Let's get our table."

Macario stayed silent until they were seated and their orders taken.

"Is that why you took today off?"

Tanner shook his head. "No. I had some personal things that couldn't wait."

Macario backed off the questioning and Tanner couldn't quite figure out if his lover believed him or just chose not to force the issue.

"Anything new on the case?" He kept his voice low.

"No." Macario shoved his hand over his hair, frustration tensing his shoulders. "He's going to take another victim soon, Tanner."

"I know. It's about that time again."

Their food arrived and they concentrated on eating for a while. Tanner had just taken his last bite when both their phones rang. Macario yanked his out and checked the number.

"It's the major."

"Go. I'll take care of the bill. I should only be a few minutes behind you."

"Okay." Macario answered his phone as he rushed out of the restaurant.

Tanner flagged down their waiter and asked for the check before dialing his own boss back.

"Tanner, we need you back at the office asap. The perp's taken another one."

"Shit. Yes, sir. I'm downtown right now. I'll be there as fast as I can."

He gave the waiter his credit card.

"Great. I'll fill you in when you get here." His boss hung up on him.

Tanner signed the slip and headed out to flag down a taxi. Hopefully Juan had screwed up and the police had been notified of the victim before Juan had got the chance to kill her. *Please don't let it be another body,* he prayed.

The task force rooms were hopping as Rangers and agents were coming in from wherever they'd gone. Tanner's boss grabbed him as he walked in. Looking around, Tanner spied Macario talking intensely to his major.

"What's up, Sam?"

"We got lucky in a way. A guy who lives in our victim's apartment building spotted a strange man carrying something from the building. He remembered the news reports, so he checked on the lady who lived on his floor."

Sam took a deep breath, causing excitement to swell in Tanner.

"And she wasn't there?"

Sam shook his head. "No. Seems our victim gave our witness a key, so he could feed her cat when she was gone. I guess when she didn't answer, he went in and found total chaos."

"Did we get prints or anything?"

"The techs are still going over the scene. Did you discover anything new after taking a closer look at the crime scene photos?"

"Yeah. Can we gather everyone? I really don't want to tell it more than once."

"Sure."

Tanner gathered his files, complete with photographs,

before heading into the room. He nodded at Macario as he made his way to the front.

"Everyone, take your seats. We're going to have a quick meeting." Major Billingsley motioned for the others to sit.

"As you've probably heard, our killer has taken another victim, but this time we have a witness and we have a chance of getting her back alive." Sam grabbed Tanner's arm and yanked him in front of the room. "Agent Wallace has some new information on our killer."

Tanner barely managed to keep from rolling his eyes. "I don't know if it means anything, but if you look at photo number six of the crime scene for each victim."

He pulled out the important photo from each grouping and pinned them to the board behind him. He'd already circled the relevant section of the victim's body.

"On each victim, carved above her left breast, is a J. I did some digging in the National Crime Database. It seems there are several unsolved crimes throughout the country that have the same J carved on the victim's body."

A phone rang and Macario frowned as he pulled his phone out. After checking the number, Macario silenced the ringer.

"Sorry."

Tanner waved off the apology. "The difference between those murders and ours is that most of the local LEOs believe their murders are drug-related."

"But we know our victims weren't involved with any sort of drug business."

He wasn't surprised that Macario spoke up. He met his lover's gaze, tilted his head in acknowledgment.

"I know that, and I'm not saying they are. I don't think drugs are the connection. I think the man doing the killing is."

A knock sounded and one of the homicide detectives not on the task force peered in.

"Guzman, there's a call for you. Said he had a hot tip, but won't talk to anyone except you."

Macario glanced at the major, who nodded. Tanner watched Macario leave while continuing to talk.

"I believe our perp works for one of the drug cartels. He enjoys killing so much, he's branching out from sanctioned killings to murder for fun. I have a note from one of the LEOs that suggested Juan Mencia. He might be a person of interest for you to look at."

"Hey, boss," one of the Rangers spoke up. "The Narcotic unit's been hearing rumors that Delarosa might have cut one of his enforcers loose."

Billingsley's narrow-eyed gaze raked the man who spoke. "Do you know which enforcer?"

"No sir."

"Then find out. Even if he's not part of this case, if we find him, we might get him to roll over on Delarosa."

Tanner stepped into the background. He'd done his job and planted the seed. The task force was intelligent enough to figure the rest out. Macario came racing back in.

"One of my informants just let me know about some weird shit happening at a warehouse on Simon Street. Something about a guy coming and going at strange times. Screaming heard a couple times."

All the men leaped to their feet, yelling as they checked their side arms.

"Wait." Billingsley's shout froze them. The older man looked at Macario. "How reliable is this informant?"

"He's never given me bad intel, sir. Also, he never comes to me unless what he knows is really fucking important."

Billingsley nodded. "Good. We need blueprints of the warehouse. As much as I'd love to ride in there like the fucking Lone Ranger, we need to smart about it. Our victim could still be alive. I don't want to risk our killer getting wind of this."

Everyone went into planning mode and Tanner stayed out of their way. He was a trained agent and could help if they needed him, but he hadn't done a lot of field work in the last year or so.

His phone beeped and he unclipped it from his belt to see he'd gotten a text. Moving to the corner, he flipped open his phone and read, '*Done*.'

Victor had come through for him. Using Macario's own informant was a stroke of genius. Nothing to connect him or his brother to the case.

When all the warrants were signed and units equipped, Tanner wandered over to Macario. His lover was strapping on a vest, and covering it with a black windbreaker that read 'Ranger' on the back.

"Take care of yourself," he said under his breath, wishing he could hug Macario, but knowing it wasn't smart to do it in the middle of police headquarters.

"I'll be as careful as I can." Macario glanced around before moving a little closer to Tanner. "Are you headed to your place?"

"I have a couple of reports to write up, but then I'll go home. I don't really need to be involved in this part of the show."

"Maybe I'll stop by if I get out before you come in tomorrow." Macario reached to squeeze Tanner's shoulder.

Tanner nodded, surprisingly touched by Macario's display of affection. "Call me after this goes down, so I know."

You're safe went unsaid.

"I will."

"Come on, Guzman. It's your informant."

Billingsley and Sam stood in the hallway, waiting for Macario. Sam met Tanner's gaze and nodded. Somehow his boss and friend had guessed Tanner's feelings for Macario.

"I'll watch his back," Sam murmured before following the others out.

"Thanks."

Sighing, Tanner strolled to his desk. It would be several hours before he heard anything and he really did have reports to write.

* * * *

Noises downstairs woke Tanner up. He slipped his hand under his pillow, gripping his handgun tightly. He climbed out of bed and froze in the doorway when he heard someone yell.

"Shit! Damn table."

Chuckling, he flicked the safety back on and left the pistol on his dresser. He tugged on a pair of sweats before heading downstairs.

"You really should have called to let me know you were coming over," he spoke as he leaned against the banister.

Macario jumped and whirled, hand reaching for his own gun before he processed it was Tanner speaking. His shoulders slumped as he dropped his hand.

"Fuck, Tanner, give me a little warning." Macario slipped out of his jacket then tossed it over the back of the recliner. He scrubbed his hands over his face. "I could've shot you."

"But you didn't." Tanner saw the exhaustion in every line of Macario's body. He held out his hand. "Come on. Let's go to bed."

Macario approached, took his hand, and pulled him into a tight embrace. Tanner encircled his lover's waist, allowing Macario to lean on him.

"We got him, Tanner."

"The woman?" He didn't know how he'd react if they'd got there too late.

"She was cut up some, but she'll live. Be years before she recovers mentally, I'm sure."

"She'll never get over it all. Probably always be afraid of the dark and strangers. Hell, her life will never be the same, but she survived and it'll make her stronger deep in her soul." Tanner had seen the pictures of the killer's victims, and he had an idea of what they'd gone through before he allowed them to die. He had no doubt it would be a very difficult process for the woman to heal.

Macario nodded and squeezed him close for a minute

before stepping back with a yawn. "I need to get a couple hours of sleep before heading back in."

They went back upstairs. Tanner stopped in the hallway and gestured to his room.

"Go and strip while I get the shower going for you."

"Damn. I should have gone home. I don't have any clothes to change into." Macario stared down at his wrinkled shirt.

"Don't worry. I probably have some stuff you can wear." Tanner gave him a gentle shove. "Now go."

"Okay."

No argument told Tanner just how tired Macario was.

"Good thing I got new underwear last week," Tanner mumbled as he turned the water on and let it warm up. He hadn't opened the underwear package yet, so Macario wouldn't be completely freaked out.

"You were right." Macario walked in, naked, and Tanner clenched his hands to keep from grabbing the man.

"Right about what?" At that second, Tanner wasn't focusing on anything other than how his lover's skin glowed under the bathroom light.

"When we dragged the perp in, some of the narcotic guys and DEA agents were there. Our guy's name is Juan Mencia. Used to work for the Delarosa cartel." Macario stepped into the shower and moaned softly as the hot water hit him.

Tanner set out clean towels. "Used to?"

"Yeah. DEA said word spread about five or six months ago that Victor Delarosa cut him loose. No one's sure why. The dealers said the word came down from the big man himself that Mencia was *persona non gratis* in any sphere of influence the kingpin controlled."

"That's why," Tanner said softly.

"Did you say something?" Macario stuck his head around the shower curtain.

"No. Finish washing up. I put out a new toothbrush for you. Do you want some briefs to wear to bed?"

"Nah. I'm good."

Tanner left Macario in the bathroom while he went back

to his bed. After stripping off his sweats and climbing under the covers, he stared at the ceiling.

Victor's cutting ties with Juan explained why his brother had given the man up without more of a fight. Tanner knew Victor would do anything for him, yet Tanner had never asked. Their mother had taught him well. Anything Victor gave him was blood money tainted by the drugs Victor sold.

Tanner sighed and rolled over to grab his personal cell phone from the nightstand.

Thank you, he text to the number he'd gotten the text from earlier.

"You get a call?"

He set his phone back down and shook his head. "Just setting a reminder for an appointment I have tomorrow."

Macario grunted as he climbed into bed. Tanner waited to see what he did. Macario reached out and tugged Tanner to him until they were spooning—Tanner's chest to Macario's back.

Tanner pressed a kiss to the nape of Macario's neck. "Sleep, love. Everything will be okay."

Macario patted Tanner's hand before falling asleep. Tanner stayed awake a little longer, wondering where everything would lead. Was there a possibility for their relationship to survive? When would be a good time to tell Macario about Victor? Or should he never mention his connection to the Delarosa cartel, hoping his lover stayed in the dark about it?

Chapter Eleven

"The defendant will stand while the verdict's read."

Tanner tensed, even having an idea of what the jury's decision would be. He worried that Juan's lawyer would find a loophole or something. Macario brushed his hand over Tanner's.

It'd been a year since they'd arrested Juan for murdering Macario's foster sister and five other women. Juan had confessed to everything, showing no remorse for what he'd done. The intriguing issue was that Juan had never once mentioned Victor or having been Victor's enforcer. Tanner wondered if the threat of death he was sure Victor had given Juan was enough to keep the man's mouth shut. Of course, there was no guarantee Juan would stay alive long enough in prison to be executed.

"We find Juan Mencia guilty of first degree murder for all six counts."

Tanner blocked out the rest as Macario took his hand and squeezed. Relief ripped through him.

"It's over," he murmured and Macario nodded.

"I need to get back to headquarters," Macario said as they made their way out of the courthouse.

"Hey, Mac," Billingsley called from where he stood with Sam. "Come here."

"I'm going to head toward the car," Tanner said.

"Okay. I'll catch up with you." Macario jogged over to the other men.

The parking lot was relatively empty. He strolled along on his own.

"Pablo?"

Tanner turned when a familiar voice called out his name. Perez strolled up to him and Tanner smiled.

"Are you back for a while?"

"A month or two. Walk with me."

Tanner nodded, knowing his brother's second-in-command wouldn't have approached him if it wasn't safe for either of them.

"He wishes for me to convey congratulations on the conviction and he wants you to know that if he had known about Juan sooner, he would have taken care of it himself."

"I know, Perez."

Perez's smile grew warmer. "Also, congratulations on your new love. He's a man you can trust and is very loyal."

Chuckling, Tanner shook his head. "I should've known he'd check out Macario."

"He loves you, Pablo, and wants only the best for you." Perez rested his hand on Tanner's arm. "I believe he wishes everyday things were different, so that you could be a family in reality."

"I wish the same thing."

And it was true. Every day he wished the past had been different and his family had never broken up, but he didn't dwell on it. Yet he was happy that he never had to deal with the dangers of being a drug lord. He didn't have the personality to survive that kind of life. So he did thank his mother for having the courage to walk away from his father.

"There's your man. I will leave you. Oh, he also wanted you to know it's white roses now."

Perez gave him a quick, hard hug before strolling away, nodding to Macario as they passed. Tanner watched as his lover's eyes widened when he realized who Perez was. Macario stopped and started to pull his gun. Tanner placed his hand on Macario's shoulder.

"Today, we let him go," he spoke softly.

"But that's..."

"Yes, it is and next time you see him, you can arrest him, but not today, love."

"Billingsley gave me the rest of the day off. Do you need to get back?" Macario shot him a narrow-eyed glare. "He hugged you."

Tanner gestured for Macario to follow him. "Let's get some takeout and I'll tell you about my family. This is something I'll only speak about once, then it'll never be brought up again."

"Okay."

They headed to their favorite Thai restaurant. Tanner had planned on telling Macario everything about his family because he loved the Texas Ranger and didn't want secrets between them anymore.

Well, he'd keep one. He'd never explain that the white roses appearing on Tanner's mother's grave came from Victor Delarosa, and served not only as a symbol of a son's love, but to let Tanner know his big brother was in town.

All the questions Macario wanted to ask crossed his face, but he refrained from asking them and Tanner appreciated it. He wasn't looking forward to spilling his guts to his lover.

They picked up their food and Macario drove them to Tanner's house.

After they'd finished eating, Macario cleaned up while Tanner grabbed two more beers from the refrigerator. They sat close together on the couch.

"Congratulations, Tanner."

He sent Macario a puzzled look. "What?"

"If you hadn't connected the J with Mencia, we might not have been able to build a case against him."

Tanner shook his head. "I just connected a few dots. Your informant came up with the warehouse."

Macario frowned. "Now that the trial is over, I can admit that man wasn't one of my informants. Or I say, he rarely gave me anything."

"Then why did you believe him?"

Macario pursed his lips and Tanner fought back the urge to kiss him.

"He described Mencia like the man stood right in front of him. My gut told me his tip was good."

"What's your informant's drug of choice?" Tanner worked on the edge of his bottle's label.

"Heroin. Why?"

"My older brother is the head of the Delarosa cartel."

He kept his gaze pinned on his bottle. Fear raced through his body as the silence grew until he thought his heart would shatter.

"Victor Delarosa is your brother?" Macario's voice was soft.

"Yes."

"Why isn't your name the same?"

Sighing, Tanner leaned back and closed his eyes. "My mother left my father when I was three. We moved to the United States legally, and she changed our names. After that, I've only seen Victor twice. The first time was when our mother died. He came to the funeral."

Macario shifted, but didn't move away from him. Tanner took that as a good sign.

"And the second time?"

He took a deep breath. "When I spotted the initial carved into the women's flesh, I knew who did it. Juan worked as an enforcer for Victor over several years."

"How did you know that if you've never seen him?"

"I've kept an eye on things." He pushed to his feet and paced. "I'm a profiler for the Bureau. I have nothing to do with the drug war or anything. I can't hurt my brother, but I won't help him either."

Macario stood then stepped into his path. His lover lifted his chin so their eyes met. Macario's hazel eyes held confusion and a struggle to understand.

"You never gave any information you heard to your brother?"

Tanner shook his head. "I'd never do that. Trust me, I thought long and hard before applying to the Bureau. I wasn't applying to any department that would give me access to information like that."

"I believe you, but what does Delarosa have to do with my informant?"

"I went to Victor and asked him if he knew where Juan was. Victor had cut Juan loose about six months before that. I'm not sure why. Victor is cold and calculating, and I'm not excusing the fact that he has no problem killing men. I know the kind of person he is. He never used to be that way."

Tanner closed his eyes, blocking out Macario's gaze for a second.

"The only thing I've noticed about Delarosa is that he doesn't kill women or children. Families seem to be off-limits to him."

That quiet observation by Macario eased something in Tanner.

"I showed Victor and Perez the crime scene photos and they recognized Juan's calling card. I asked if they knew where he was."

"Your brother handed me that information through a snitch," Macario commented.

Tanner nodded. "I think so. Victor knows about you and me. To keep me out from under any kind of scrutiny, you were the logical person to contact. He wouldn't risk either of our careers by contacting us personally."

"He gave Mencia up without being forced. Doesn't he worry that Mencia might try to lessen his sentence by rolling over on him?"

Tanner eased away and started to pace again, drinking from his bottle. "It certainly doesn't seem so, does it? Juan could have done it before we went to trial. I wouldn't be surprised that Victor threatened him, and I don't doubt that if it came down to it, Victor could reach him, no matter where he ended up. In fact, I have a feeling Mencia won't make it to his execution."

Stopping, he stared out of his front window. Not caring what was happening outside, he studied Macario's reflection in the glass. His lover's head lowered and Macario tucked his hands in his pockets.

"I know you'll need to think about all of this. I want you to believe me. Once Mother and I got here, we cut all ties to my father and Victor. Mother worked two jobs to support us. When I was old enough, I worked. I paid my own way through college. I haven't taken any money or anything else from Victor." He shoved his hands through his hair. "I wish it was different. I wish I could visit my brother. I want to be able to admit I have a brother. It's lonely not having any family. I have very few memories of the time I used to live on the compound in Mexico, but the things I do remember are times I spent playing with Victor. He was so much fun. It hurts to see what he's become, and knowing he was the one sacrificed to my father's need for an heir."

Macario approached him and embraced him, wrapping him tight to his chest. Macario nuzzled his hair.

"I do need to think about all this, Tanner, but never doubt you have family. There are people who care deeply for you, and I get the feeling that Victor cares for you as well, or he could have made your life hell." Macario paused briefly, then continued, "Delarosa is an example of how bad people can do good things from time to time."

Tanner leaned back and let Macario support him for a moment. After a few seconds, he stepped away.

"You should probably go before I start begging you to stay." Tanner tried to smile, but failed. "You have my number. Call me when you reach a decision."

"I will."

Tanner watched Macario walk away. He kept the tears at bay for the rest of the day until he climbed in bed alone that night. Curled around the pillow that still smelled like Macario, he cried.

Tanner had never felt so alone, not even when his mother had died. All he could do was have faith that Macario believed him, and still loved him, even after finding out who Tanner's brother was.

His phone buzzed, and Tanner snatched it off the table next to the bed. He couldn't help the hint of disappointment when he saw it wasn't Macario's number. Yet when he read the text, he smiled.

Don't worry about anything, little brother. I'll take care of this.

Don't hurt him.

Tanner sent his text, then lay back to stare at the ceiling. His cell vibrated, and he checked what came through.

Would I be so dumb as to do something like that? Get some sleep. Things will be better in the morning.

Good night.

He fell asleep, tears still falling from his eyes.

* * * *

Macario sat in his apartment, no lights on, allowing his thoughts to wander. How did he reconcile everything he knew about Tanner with the knowledge that Tanner's brother was one of the most powerful drug lords in the Americas?

He'd run across Victor Delarosa and Victor's second-in-command, Perez. Both men were handsome in a cold, snake-like way. Power and self-confidence rolled off Delarosa. The man thought he was invincible and so far, it'd been true. Neither the Rangers nor any Federal agency had been able to pin anything on the man.

If Macario had been more suspicious, he'd believe Tanner spied for his brother, but he trusted his lover. Tanner had said he'd never given Delarosa any tips or information. Tanner's inability to lie made Macario fairly certain Tanner knew nothing about Delarosa's network.

Would he be able to love Tanner and not try to use the

man's connection to snare Delarosa? That became the most important question. Taking down a drug cartel should be top on Macario's list of professional goals. Yet he knew how betrayed Tanner would be if he used him like that.

A sharp knock on his door brought him out of his thoughts. He climbed to his feet and went to the door. Checking the peephole first, he stiffened at the sight of Perez, Delarosa's right-hand man, standing in the hallway.

"Fuck," he whispered.

"Ranger Guzman, I know you're in there. Please, open the door. We mean you no harm."

Something in Perez's voice commanded Macario to obey. They knew he and Tanner were lovers. Neither Perez nor Delarosa would kill him, if only to spare Tanner pain.

Wishing he still wore his gun, he unlocked the door and swung it open. Perez pushed in, followed closely by Victor Delarosa. Macario fell back, giving ground to the two men.

"Macario Guzman, I'm Perez and this is my boss, Victor Delarosa."

Perez's rather formal introduction surprised Macario. He nodded to them.

"Please, I only wish to speak to you. Nothing more." Delarosa motioned between Perez and himself. "That is why Perez alone accompanies me."

"I didn't think you were in Houston." Strange comment, but his mind was processing the situation slowly.

"I've been in Houston for several months now, though it's getting close to migration time for us. I'm not fond of Houston in the summer."

Delarosa glanced around the dimly lit living room. He spied the couch and took a seat. Perez stood behind him, silently guarding his boss.

"Would you like something to drink?"

"I would enjoy a glass of water."

"Mr. Perez?" Macario asked.

"Water would be fine as well."

After going into the kitchen, Macario marveled at the

surrealism he was in the middle of right then. He should be calling for backup to come and arrest Delarosa, but he couldn't. The man had come in good faith, wanting nothing more than to talk.

He got three bottles of water out of the refrigerator and two glasses from the cupboard. Somehow he couldn't see the elegant Delarosa swigging water from a plastic bottle. Macario played the good host, making sure Delarosa and his man were taken care of. When that was done, he sat and stared at the drug lord, wondering what would happen now.

"You know who I am by now," Delarosa said.

"Yes, sir. Tanner told me earlier today."

"Ah, Pablo is an honest man. So refreshing in today's world." Delarosa's grin held fondness for his younger brother.

"Pablo?" Macario couldn't help but ask.

"Tanner's real name. Or maybe I should say his original name. When our mother brought him here, she changed their names. She wanted nothing to tie them to our father."

This time Delarosa's smile was sad.

"Can't really blame her. She sounds like a strong woman," Macario muttered, not sure what he was supposed to say.

"Mama was. After she had Pablo, she began to wish for a different life. The mansions and clothes were all well and good, but they were bought with blood money. She hated the bodyguards and not being able to trust anyone."

Macario imagined it might have been trying at times.

"She didn't know what my father did until after they were married. She loved him very much, yet she couldn't accept how he made his money. When Pablo turned three, a rival cartel tried to kidnap him. That is when she said no more. She couldn't justify risking her sons' lives for the money the drugs brought in."

Macario shifted slightly in his chair. "I'm surprised your father let her go. From what I've heard, he didn't take kindly to people leaving."

Delarosa chuckled coldly. "My father was psychotic and quite happy to kill whenever the mood struck him. Yet, as odd as it might seem, he loved my mother. Seeing her unhappy broke his heart. He let her go with Pablo with the only stipulation being that I had to stay with him."

"Knowing how tender-hearted Tanner is, I imagine it hurt your mother terribly to leave you behind."

Delarosa didn't speak for a moment. Eventually he nodded. "You're right. Pablo told me she was never the same after they left Mexico."

"Why tell me this?" Macario gestured vaguely between them. "What does that have to do with us?"

"Everything. I came to tell you that Pablo is loyal and steadfast. He's always known when I'm in Houston. He's never told his fellow agents. Yet I'm sure there have been times when he's come across information that would help me. He's never called or done anything to give me a heads-up." Delarosa paused. "He has called after the fact to make sure I'm okay."

Unable to sit any longer, Macario stood and paced in front of Delarosa who watched him with understanding eyes. That was something Macario never thought he'd say about Victor Delarosa, that he had kind eyes. Perez stayed silent, a quiet observer.

"I keep an eye on Pablo, merely to make sure he's okay. I don't interfere usually. I thought this time it might be necessary."

"Why would it be necessary?" Macario stopped and glanced at Delarosa, who snorted.

"I told you I keep an eye on my brother. He cares about you very much. So much in fact, that he came to me for help with Juan last year. If he hadn't been worried about you, he would've never risked everything to see me."

"My foster sister was one of Mencia's victims," Macario confessed.

"I know. Because Pablo has never asked me for anything, I chose to help him."

"By throwing Mencia to the wolves."

It was Perez's turn to snort, causing Macario to meet the man's gaze. He was surprised to see the humor shining in his eyes.

"Juan was a problem I no longer felt like dealing with. Admittedly, I would have gotten more mileage out of him if I'd had him killed, but sometimes what's good for business might not be good for other people." Delarosa picked a piece of lint off his slacks.

"Who?"

Delarosa shrugged.

"For the victims' families. Closure is good in cases such as these." Perez spoke up for the first time since arriving at Macario's apartment.

"None of my reasons matter. What's important is that you judge my brother by his own actions, not by who his family is, because he would never betray either of us." Delarosa stood and held out his hand. "This will be the only time we talk, Macario Guzman. I'm entrusting you with something far more precious to me than my empire. Treat Pablo well, and I'll have no problems with you."

"Thank you, and I will." Macario shook Victor Delarosa's hand before escorting them to the door.

"I'm sure you'll be calling your friends at the DEA when we're gone," Victor said, and Macario couldn't deny it. "Good. You're an excellent police officer, Guzman. I would expect nothing less from you."

After shutting and locking it behind Delarosa and Perez, Macario leaned back against it. That had to be one of the strangest encounters he'd ever had. Yet in a way, it made him glad to know that Delarosa had Tanner's back, no matter what.

He checked the clock and decided it was too late to call Tanner. He'd call him in the morning and they'd begin the rest of their lives together. But first he had to make a phone call to Snap about Victor, and he tried to ignore how having Victor's blessing eased his guilt a little.

* * * *

Macario stared at his phone for a second before returning it to his ear. "Agent Wallace resigned?"

MacLaughlin exhaled loudly. "Yes. My best profiler up and quit. His resignation was on my desk yesterday before we knew the outcome of the trial. I knew Tanner hadn't been happy for a while, but I never thought he'd quit without coming to see me first."

"That's surprising, sir. I'll try his cell phone. Thank you."

Hanging up, Macario struggled to make sense of Tanner's resignation. Why would he do that?

"I'm heading out for lunch," he informed Billingsley as he walked by the man's office.

"Okay." He acknowledged Macario with a wave.

Before he could get out of the building, he heard his name called. He turned to watch Snap stroll up to him.

"Hey, Mac, wanted to thank you for the tip about Delarosa. Unfortunately, he wasn't at his place when we got there." Snap shook his head. "I'm starting to think he's a damned ghost."

"Oh, he's real, and all his competitors would say that as well. He'll screw up at some point, and you'll catch him." He slapped Snap on the shoulder. "I'll call you later this week, and we'll set up another poker game. It's been a while since I've taken your money, my friend. What the hell are you doing here anyway?"

"Have to talk with your boss about another case that just dropped into my lap." Snap's bright grin brought a smile from Mac. "Talk to you later."

Macario felt a little guilty for letting the DEA know Victor was back in town, but he had to do his job, and he didn't think Tanner would be too upset with him. His lover understood what being a Ranger meant to him. He waited until he was in his car before he called Tanner's cell. He tapped his fingers on the steering wheel as he listened to it ring.

"Hello."

"Why the hell didn't you tell me you quit the Bureau?"

Okay. He might have approached that a little more diplomatically.

"I meant to, but it slipped my mind while I was explaining about Victor."

"Why did you quit, Tanner? I thought you liked working for the Bureau."

He started his car and pulled into traffic, knowing where he was headed without making a conscious decision.

"I've been a profiler for eight years, Macario. You've done homicides. You know how all those bodies can wear on you. I'm tired of the nightmares. I want to do something different."

"What? Have you given it any thought?"

"Yes. I've applied for a position at a center for teens. It specializes in helping gay teenagers who find themselves abandoned by their families." Tanner sounded excited.

Macario turned on Tanner's street. "You're having company for lunch."

"I am? Who?"

"Me."

He hung up and parked the car before climbing out. Tanner stood in the doorway as he approached. They looked at each other until Tanner finally nodded and turned to go inside.

"I was going to grill a steak. Since you'll be eating the one I planned to have for dinner, you'll have to bring something home with you tonight."

"Okay."

Macario didn't broach the subject again until lunch was ready and they sat to eat.

"Why did you become an agent? I thought you said you always wanted to be in law enforcement."

Tanner shoved his steak around his plate. "The more I think about it, the more I believe I was trying to balance out the bad stuff my father and brother have done."

"But none of that had anything to do with you. You shouldn't be atoning for your brother's sins," Macario protested.

"I know that now. It took me a while to figure it out. There are a lot of kids living on the streets because their parents throw them out and a lot of those kids are hooked on drugs. I want to balance out the bad with something that isn't going to drive me to a nervous breakdown."

When Tanner met Macario's gaze, his eyes were bleak and full of pain.

"I don't want to deal with dead people anymore. I want to hope that I can help someone before it's too late."

Macario thought about it. Being a cop could be hard sometimes. It was too easy to become cynical and distrusting of everyone, even your friends. There was a softness in Tanner that Macario never wanted his love to lose. If he continued working for the Bureau, Tanner would become hard and cold or he'd break. Macario didn't want either of those happening.

"You're right," he agreed aloud. "You need to bring hope to the living. I'll support you in whatever way you need me."

"As a friend or a lover?" Tanner didn't seem certain he wanted to know the answer to his question.

"As a partner, Pablo."

Tanner's dark eyes widened at Macario's use of his real name.

"You talked to Victor," Tanner said softly.

"Your older brother paid me a visit last night and did his best to convince me you were an honest man."

Ducking his head, Tanner refused to meet his gaze. "I'm sorry."

"Don't be. Delarosa obviously cares a great deal about you and he wants to see you happy. Lucky for me, I feel the same way, so he had no reason to harm me. But you do realize that I can't ignore that you know where he is."

Tanner shook his head. "I don't always know when he's

in town, and even if I did and told you, he'd be gone before you got there. Victor doesn't expect me to lie to keep him safe. He has his own ways of doing it."

Not wanting to talk about Victor anymore, Macario stood then walked around the table before kneeling next to Tanner. He took the man's hands in his and smiled.

"I love you, Tanner Wallace. It doesn't matter who your family is or what they do. I see only you."

Tears welled in Tanner's eyes and he fell into Macario's arms. Macario kissed his lover, turning it into a pledge. Tanner tugged at Macario's tie and he let Tanner start stripping him. It didn't matter if he was late getting back from lunch. All that did matter was Macario proving to Tanner with every touch, word, and deed how much he loved him. Macario figured it would take a lifetime to do so.

Epilogue

As they strolled through the cemetery, Tanner fought the urge to take Macario's hand in his. While he was out at his new job, he knew Macario wasn't, and his lover never really liked public displays of affection any way.

He looked around, noticing there were a few other people in the area, and he couldn't help wondering if they worked for his brother in some way. Tanner wouldn't have been surprised to find out Victor had men shadowing him and Macario. Since Tanner wasn't in the FBI anymore, Victor considered him more vulnerable to attacks from his brother's enemies.

Tanner tried to convince him that he was still quite capable to handle any situation, plus no one aside from Macario knew Tanner was Victor's younger brother. It wasn't likely they'd discover it unless someone told them.

"Your sister is buried close to my mother," he said.

Tanner glanced over at Macario. It was the first time his lover had visited the cemetery since they'd buried Marissa a year ago. It had struck Tanner as fate when he'd realized how close the two of them were.

"How did that happen?" Macario studied him with a skeptical look on his face.

Shrugging, Tanner shoved his hands in his pockets. "Just the way things worked out. I doubt very much Victor played any role in this."

"I'm not putting anything past your brother, considering who he is."

"Probably a good thing." He veered on the right hand path, heading toward Marissa's burial site.

Macario's face was pale and his hands shook slightly. Tanner didn't comment on that. Macario was still coming to terms with Marissa's violent death. Even though her killer had been caught, it would take years for Macario to fully integrate her loss into his life.

A frown creased Macario's forehead as they approached Marissa's headstone. "Who put flowers on her grave?"

Tanner noticed the bouquet and he stumbled to a halt. A dozen white roses glowed in the early morning sun. If he were to visit his mother's grave, he'd find another dozen.

"I don't know."

But he did know. Victor was back in town and by putting flowers on Marissa's grave, he was informing Tanner that Macario was a part of the family now, plus giving him his approval to Tanner and Macario's relationship.

Tanner silently thanked his brother before putting Victor out of his mind. It was time to embrace Macario and offer a shoulder to cry on, if that was what he needed, because Tanner always believed love meant standing by the person you cared for no matter what.

Snap Decision

Excerpt

Chapter One

"Hey, Jefferson," Epstein, one of D'Marcus 'Snap' Jefferson's fellow DEA agents yelled to him.

"What?" he shouted back without looking up from his computer.

"Some guy is here from Customs and Border Patrol. Says he has something that might interest you." Epstein's raised voice held disbelief.

Snap felt kind of the same way, but he couldn't blow the guy off. He never knew when he might be working with the CBP and it paid to have a good relationship with them.

"All right. I'll be right there."

"I put him in Interrogation Two," Epstein told him.

He grunted in reply, doing his best to get his report done before he went to talk to the guy. One of the few things that pissed him off about being an agent—and a cop in general—was all the damn paperwork. Even now that most of the forms were on computer and he didn't have to write them up by hand, he still hated having to spend part of his day at his desk, trying to justify why he had done what he did, or trying to explain why they'd failed to catch Victor Delarosa yet again.

Snap hit save then send. Standing, he lifted his arms above his head and stretched, listening as his spine cracked and creaked. Dalton Lillien, his partner, laughed.

"You're getting old, man. Soon you'll be promoted to a permanent desk job," Dalton joked.

"I'll retire before that happens. Go get a cushy sheriff's job somewhere in Montana."

"Montana? Dude, you wouldn't be able to handle the winters up there. You're a Southern boy born and bred. Your blood's too thin for snow and ice." Dalton hooted in amusement.

Flipping him the finger was the only reply Snap made as he turned to head to the interrogation room. *Why would Border Patrol come all the way here to talk to me? Why not just call me?* It could have something to do with the Delarosa case, but still Snap figured it would have just been easier to call.

As he approached the room, a guy stepped out of it, and Snap grinned. "Amirez, what the hell did you bring me?"

Agent Amirez was a long-time friend of Snap's and now that he knew who it was, he had a feeling that whatever Amirez had brought him was going to be important.

"Snap," Amirez said, holding out his hand. "It's good to see you. Someday I'm going to have to get back up here when it's not business."

"Yeah. You've missed a few poker games."

They shook hands then Amirez gestured to the door behind him.

"I brought you something interesting to puzzle out. You guys get to figure out whether he's telling the truth or not."

"Who?"

He led the way to the small room to the right of the main interrogation area, then looked through the one-way glass at the man sitting at the table. He was younger than Snap and had dark brown hair that curled around his ears. When the guy glanced up as though he knew Snap was watching him, Snap swore.

"What? Do you know him?"

"No, but he looks like someone I do know. What's his story?"

Amirez pulled out a notebook and flipped through some pages until he found what he was looking for. "Yesterday evening, around nine, he showed up at the Veterans border crossing in Brownsville and was pulled out of line to be searched. Once they took him into the office, he said that he had some information about some drug movements over the border. When the agents pressed, he said he wouldn't talk to anyone but you."

Snap frowned. "Me? I don't know who he is. Why would he ask for me?"

"I don't know, man. He stopped talking after that. I was running up here for a meeting with the Rangers, so I got volunteered to bring him to you. Just keep us in the loop." Amirez slapped Snap on the back. "I've got to head out or I'll be late."

"I'll be contacting them myself in a few." Snap had a feeling he was going to need to talk to one particular Ranger. He followed his friend out before he went to find his supervisor. After he knocked on his boss's door, he stuck his head in. "I need to discuss something with you. Can you come with me?"

Penn stood without saying a word, joining Snap who also gestured for Dalton to come with them. As they returned to the observation room, he filled them in on what Amirez had told him.

"Why did you want me here? Just go in and talk to him. I don't know if he'll have anything, but if he's willing to talk to you, then take advantage of it." Penn folded his arms over his chest and glared at him.

"I want to get permission to bring the Rangers in on this," he informed his boss.

Dalton gave him a narrow-eyed stare, then turned to look at the man in the other room. When the guy lifted his head from where he'd laid it on the table, Dalton grunted.

"Do you see it?" Snap wanted to make sure he wasn't crazy.

"Yeah. I get why you want to contact the Rangers. Calling Guzman, huh?"

After glancing between them, Penn huffed in annoyance. "Fine. It's nice to see that you two know what's going on. Go ahead and call the Rangers. If you get some flak, have them contact me."

"Thank you, sir." Snap waited until Penn left before he pulled out his phone to call Guzman. "It's uncanny how much they look alike."

"Yet there are differences. This guy looks like he's lived some hard years in his life. I'd say he's a year or two older than Tanner." Dalton propped his hip on the edge of the desk.

Snap nodded, listening to the phone ring.

"Guzman," a hard voice answered.

"Mac, it's Snap. How's it going?"

Mac chuckled. "As good as it can be hunting bad guys. How are you doing, Snap? Bust any drug dealers lately?"

"All the time, but not the big one yet." Snap and Macario 'Mac' Guzman had been friends for a long time, ever since Mac had moved to Houston from California and started working with the Rangers.

"Well, Delarosa has managed to survive the cutthroat world of a drug lord for this long. I'm pretty sure it's going to take better men than you and me to take him down," Mac commiserated.

Snap sniffed. "I plan on taking the man down before I retire and if you're nice to me, I might give you some credit when the time comes."

Mac's laugh held disbelief, yet he didn't tell Snap he was crazy. "What can I do for you? You aren't calling to cancel dinner, are you?"

"No. I'll be there at six on Saturday. This is a work call. I probably should've gone through official channels, but I want you to see something. Once you get a look, then you can decide how to handle getting you involved with what I'm doing." Snap let his gaze wander to the stranger waiting for him. "My gut's telling me something weird is going on. Can you come over to the DEA offices?"

"Sure. I can be there in ten. Have to finish up some paperwork first, or Cap will hunt me down."

Snap got a mental image of Mac rolling his eyes and he laughed. "Paperwork will be the death of us all. I'll let Cook know you're heading over—that way you can come on up without having to have them call me first."

"Thanks. See you in a few." Mac hung up.

He put his phone back in its holder on his belt. Propping his hands on his hips, he kept his focus on the man.

"Who are you?" he murmured.

"Go on in and ask. I'll go out and wait for Mac. If what this guy knows is time sensitive, we need to get all the information we can from him." Dalton poked him in the side as he walked by. "Be careful. He looks rather fragile."

He looks like an addict who's coming down from a three-day high. Snap didn't like the way those elegant hands shook or those bloodshot brown eyes. Straightening his shoulders, Snap put on his game face. He couldn't show any sympathy or pity for the informant. It would be too easy to be manipulated if he empathized with him.

"I'm Agent D'Marcus Jefferson. You wanted to talk to me?" He shut the door behind him after stepping in.

I'm in so much trouble. Kenneth Santos swallowed as the largest man he'd ever seen walked into the room. The space around him seemed to shrink until it was as though all the air had been sucked out, and Ken's lungs burned as he panted.

Christ! He wanted a hit so bad, but kept telling himself that that part of his life was over. He had fought so hard to get clean, and by some grace of God, he was being given a chance to clear his slate with one particular cartel.

"What's your poison?"

Jumping halfway out of his chair when Agent Jefferson spoke, Ken braced his hands on the table to keep from falling to the floor. The blank expression on the agent's face told Ken that the man had seen it all before.

"What do you mean?" He didn't want to admit to anything, though he was pretty sure Jefferson had had him pegged the moment he'd looked at him through the glass.

"You're coming down and jonesing for a hit. What's your poison?"

"Why? You going out to score me some?" Ken could've smacked himself in the face when he heard the snotty—yet hopeful—tone in his voice.

Jefferson shot him a 'you've got to be kidding' look. "Do I look like the guy you send out to score drugs?"

No! You look like the guy the cartel sends out to break bones and kill people. There was no way he was going to say that to the DEA agent, though. He rubbed his hands on his pants. When he noticed how Jefferson stiffened when his hands went under the table, Ken quickly brought them back into view.

"Sorry. I don't have anything. The Border Patrol guy made sure I wasn't carrying a weapon." He licked his lips, wishing he had a glass of water or something.

The narrow stare Jefferson gave him caused Ken's stomach to clench. God, he'd only seen colder eyes once before in his life and he never wanted to see that man again.

"Heroin and cocaine," he blurted. A slow blink was all he got in response to his confession. "I mean, that's what I used to take. I've been clean for six months, you know, but I still haven't gotten rid of the cravings. Maybe I'll always look like I'm coming off a high."

"Maybe—"

Jefferson was interrupted by a knock on the door.

He moved toward it, and Ken took a deep breath. It was easier to breathe without the big man looming over him. He entwined his fingers and gripped them tight. *Ken, you need to stop fidgeting. He knows you have something to tell him, and it's not like you don't have permission to spill your secrets. It's the only way you're going to be free forever.*

"What the fuck?"

Ken shot to his feet at the shout and backed away from the angry voice. The chair hit the floor behind him, tangling up with his legs, and he fell, arms flailing. Before he landed, he was snatched up and set back on his feet at such speed it drew a gasp from him.

When his vision steadied, he found himself getting an up close and personal view of Jefferson's eyes. They weren't completely brown like he'd originally thought. There were streaks of gold swirling through the darkness that fascinated him.

"You okay?"

Again, the harsh voice that had started his rather embarrassing performance startled him and he jerked.

"Jesus, man. Take a pill or something."

Jefferson smirked. "I think his problem is he's taken too many of them. His nerves are shot."

While Ken knew he deserved the snide comments because of his life choices, he didn't appreciate being made fun of like that. He yanked his arms away from Jefferson then bent to pick up the chair. He settled into it with as much dignity as he could manage before he looked at the newcomer.

"Who are you?"

After setting his white Stetson on the table, the man braced his hands on the surface as he leaned into Ken's personal space. "I was about to ask you the same thing."

Knowing he didn't really have any bargaining chips, Ken decided to bluff as much as he could. "I said I'd only talk to Agent Jefferson."

"Yes, we're aware of your conditions, but, you see, you don't hold any real cards here, my friend. We can kick you to the curb any time we want." Jefferson crossed his arms over his massive chest, straining the T-shirt he wore.

And that was the problem. Ken couldn't be ignored, or he would've failed in his mission and he was as good as dead then. Ken might have lived most of his life as though he was trying to kill himself, but he didn't really want to die. The urge to live had been why he'd started cleaning himself up.

"Let's try this again. Who are you?" the Texas Ranger asked.

Ken recognized the traditional cowboy hat the Rangers wore. He frowned, not sure why the DEA would call in a Ranger for something like this. "I'm Kenneth Santos. I'm an American citizen and I have information on drug shipments."

"Santos, huh?" Jefferson stepped forward and clicked on the microphone in the middle of the table. "Say that again."

Ken repeated himself, knowing someone was running a background check on him. It wasn't an interesting life he'd led. Mostly one of squandered opportunities. It wasn't like he'd been an abused child or anything like that. His mother and stepdad had done all they could to keep him away from the path he'd chosen.

"I'm Lieutenant Macario Guzman, and I work with the DEA from time to time." Guzman relaxed slightly, which eased a little of the tension in the room. "Do you know a Tanner Wallace?"

Running through his memories—drug-fogged as they were—he shook his head. "The name doesn't sound familiar. Why?"

"None of your business at the moment." Guzman tilted his head toward the door as he looked at Jefferson. "I need to talk to you."

Jefferson nodded then said to Ken, "I'll have someone bring you some coffee and a jacket."

Chapter Two

Snap didn't know why he'd agreed to let Ken have those things, but he could tell that the man was freezing. He wore a long-sleeved T-shirt, but it had holes and was ragged around the edges. It was clean, though, which was a plus. And his jeans had tears at the knees. Everything Ken wore spoke of being down as far as a man could go, yet still trying to hang onto some pride—or maybe trying to get some self-respect back.

He flagged down Dalton and asked his partner to get a jacket and some coffee for Ken. Then he turned to look at Mac.

"You do see why I called you, right?"

Mac nodded. "He's the spitting image of Tanner, but I don't know how that's possible. Tanner doesn't have any family."

Snap snorted. "Kenneth Santos just might be the prodigal son. Maybe Tanner's dad had a wandering eye."

Mac winced and Snap wondered what that was about. "He could've, but Tanner didn't know his dad. From what he said, his parents divorced when Tanner was three and he never saw his dad after that."

"Is the old man still alive?" Snap should've been in there, badgering Ken to give up all his secrets, but he wanted to figure out how Kenneth Santos could look exactly like his friend's lover as well.

"No." Mac's answer was definite.

"Damn." He rubbed the back of his neck. "Okay. We'll have to table that discussion for another time. I need to start questioning him. You want to be in there with me?"

Mac shifted on his feet while he thought. "Yes. I'm going to call Cap and tell him what's going on."

Snap turned to go back. "Are you going to call Tanner?"

"Not until we know more about Mr. Santos. It might be a coincidence. I mean everyone is supposed to have a doppelganger out there. He could be Tanner's."

Something in the tone of Mac's voice told Snap the man didn't believe that. He clasped Mac's shoulder hard then returned to the interrogation room. Dalton handed him a few sheets of paper before he went in.

Ken looked up when Snap stepped in. His lips didn't have the blue tinge to them that had prompted Snap to get a jacket for him. Whoever Dalton had borrowed it from was obviously much bigger than Ken because it swamped him. His hands weren't shaking as badly as they had been, and he had them wrapped around the coffee mug.

"All right, Mr. Santos," Snap said as he settled into the chair across the table from Ken. He scanned the information on the papers while Ken eyed him nervously.

He knew he was rather imposing. At six-seven and two hundred and thirty pounds, he'd scared even hardened criminals while busting in doors during raids. He kept his head shaved, which he knew added to the overall look, and he liked it that way.

When he and Dalton questioned witnesses and dealers, he usually stood in the corner glowering at them while Dalton played the sympathetic role. It was a partnership that had worked well so far.

Interestingly, while Ken watched him as though he was a hawk and Ken was the prey, the man didn't move. He sipped his coffee, acting for the most part like nothing was wrong.

"I see this isn't your first time being questioned by law enforcement," Snap commented.

"No, sir," Ken answered, but didn't elaborate.

Snap glanced up at him, meeting Ken's dark brown eyes. "Care to explain?"

Shrugging, Ken stared at the microphone that Snap had turned on again when he'd come in. "Why should I? I'm sure my record is obvious to an experienced agent like you. I was a good kid until I started using. Then my life went to shit and I fucked up."

"I'm trying to understand something here." Snap tapped his finger on the top page. "You got out of prison after doing three years for drug possession. You seem to have cleaned up your life, working a steady job and keeping your nose out of the coke. As far as I can see, you haven't shot heroin again—or at least haven't been caught doing it."

Ken shook his head. "No. I've been clean for six months. It was a month after I got out that I decided to straighten up and dry out. I was still getting high while I was inside."

Snap wasn't surprised at that news. As hard as the guards tried, they couldn't get all the drugs out of the system and if a prisoner knew how to play the game, they could get anything they wanted.

"What made you change your habits?" Snap tugged a pen from the side pocket on his black cargo pants. He flipped one of the sheets over, ready to take notes.

Before Ken said anything, Mac came in. He set his hat on a chair in the corner then joined Snap at the table. He sat, but didn't say anything, so Snap motioned for Ken to continue.

It had to have been obvious to Ken that Mac was staying and he wasn't going to be able to talk to Snap alone. Ken sighed, wiggled a second in his seat, then said, "I decided I didn't want to die."

Mac snorted. "Man, there are thousands of junkies out there who decide every other month they don't want to die, so they quit for a day. When the withdrawals hit and they're puking their guts up, they run out to get more shit. What makes you so special that you've made it, what, six months?"

Ken dropped his gaze to the mug in his hands. "I'm not special. I never tried to quit before because I didn't want to. Now that I do, it's a constant struggle. I've had to rearrange my entire life. Move away and cut ties with all my old friends. Every morning I wake up in pain, craving heroin and coke."

Snap understood how hard it was to go cold turkey. In one of his first undercover jobs, he'd come very close to being addicted to coke. Thank God they'd gotten the evidence they needed before he had to do too much of it. Yet he'd had to go through rehab to kick the habit. It hadn't been fun. He couldn't imagine how difficult it was for Ken to drag his ass out of bed with that hunger eating at his soul.

"Okay. If you aren't doing any shit, then exactly what kind of information can you give me on drug shipments? Are you a mule for one of the cartels?" Snap saw the small wince Ken gave at the mention of the cartels. He also noticed how tense Mac had become as well.

"Yeah, I did transport smaller shipments," Ken confessed. "I was on their radar, though for bigger stuff, I'm sure. I had been getting desperate before I got arrested. I was contacted a week ago about doing some more of that for them. I refused, but you know how it goes with a cartel. You don't say no to them."

"So they want you to transport drugs for them again?" Mac said.

"Yes." Ken nodded, turning the cup around and around in his hands. "They found me here in Dallas. I'd moved from California, hoping they would just leave me alone, but I guess I was one of their better mules. They searched me out."

Snap rocked back on the rear two legs of his chair, ignoring the ominous creaking of the metal. He tapped the pen against his bottom lip for a moment while staring at Ken. "See, that's what doesn't make sense to me. The Cortez cartel is one of the most violent drug suppliers—if not *the* most violent. I think they took over that dubious distinction from the Delarosa cartel. Yet you're willing to risk your life. Actually not just your life, but those of your parents and relatives. Why?"

Mac took up from there. "Right. Why risk their lives? You know they aren't going to come after *you* if they find out you're meeting with the DEA. The cartels are all about making a statement and you'll be finding body parts on your doorstep within a day."

"You're right. Except I don't have any family left. It's in that file you're building on me. My parents died when I was in college and my younger brother died three years ago in the war. I only have the people I used to hang out with, and trust me, none of them are people I'll mourn if they were to die." Ken shivered, wrapping the edges of the jacket around his slender body.

Well, that was sad. Snap knew his parents were going to die at some point. He was just hoping they had several more years left to annoy him and his sisters. He loved his nephews and nieces. They were part of the reason why he did his job. A world without drugs might be too much to hope for, but he was doing his best to keep as much as possible off the streets and away from children.

He didn't let his feelings show, not wanting Mac or Ken to know he was slightly sympathetic at this point. "Why ask for me? I'm a thorn in the cartels' sides. I'm sure they curse my name every chance they get. Is that why you decided to come looking for me?"

More books from T.A. Chase

Book one in the Home series

Six years ago, a hoof to the head ended his career and his relationship with the man he loved.

Book one in the Rags to Riches series

Finding a solution for his boss brings Ion to the point of having his deepest fantasies come true.

Book one in the Beasor Chronicles

Will the unconditional love of his best friend be enough to help heal Percy after almost being broken?

Book one in the Four Horsemen series

For Pestilence, the White Horseman, love becomes the most powerful cure.

About the Author

T.A. Chase

There is beauty in every kind of love, so why not live a life without boundaries? Experiencing everything the world offers fascinates TA and writing about the things that make each of us unique is how she shares those insights. When not writing, TA's watching movies, reading and living life to the fullest.

T.A. Chase loves to hear from readers. You can find contact information, website details and an author profile page at https://www.pride-publishing.com/